Percy Fitz

and the

Alien Artifact

Adventures of Percy Fitz Series

Book One – *Percy Fitz and the Hidden Kingdom*

Book Two – *Percy Fitz and the Dome of Doom*

Book Three – *Percy Fitz and the Measureless Cavern*

Book Four – *Percy Fitz and the Aztec Treasure*

Book Five – *Percy Fitz and the Green Man Mystery*

Book Six – *Percy Fitz and the Alien Artifact*

Percy Fitz

and the

Alien Artifact

D. E. Wilson

Self-Published by D. E. Wilson

Cover art by Justin Britton

First published through CreateSpace in 2016 from a 2012 manuscript.

Percy Fitz and the Alien Artifact is Book Six in the *Adventures of Percy Fitz Series.*

Chapter 1

A bookmark, or something else?

When Percy Fitz found the bookmark in a volume of Aurora history laying on his night stand, it changed everything. I mean, it changed what was to happen in the near future, because, you see, it wasn't really a bookmark. It was a . . . but wait, I'm getting ahead of our story. We have to go back a number of cycles. (Cycles are how they measure time in the Aurora Dome. Three cycles equal 24 hours, or what we would call a day.) We have to go back to the time when the Green Man left Aurora.

The Green Man had just left. He had stood in the courtyard of Aurora Castle, adjusted his Transporter Gens and MiniGen and pressed a button. The invisible transporter room enveloped him, and, with a popping noise and bright light, he disappeared. Percy and Princess Portia both went to their rooms feeling sad and uneasy. They both said after he left that they

1

should have gone with him to help find his uncle. He was sure to get in trouble by himself. How a man from such a technologically-advanced planet could be such a, such a dunderhead, was a mystery. ("Dunderhead" is what Percy's grandfather would have called someone as disorganized and careless as the Green Man.)

He never took anything seriously. He'd get excited, but never get worried or alarmed. And he could never focus on any one thing for very long. Percy shuttered when he remembered all the trouble he had caused while in the Netherworld kingdom of Aurora. He had trapped himself in solid stone, then trapped Percy, Portia, and the mountain family in there with him. Then he had transported them all to a terrifying pit called The Rings. They all would have frozen to death in that lake of ice at the bottom of The Rings if it hadn't been for Percy and Portia. (Those of you who haven't read *Percy Fitz and the Green Man Mystery*, won't, of course, know what I'm talking about.) Even then, when the ceiling of the transporter room was about to cave in, the Green Man wasn't overly alarmed. Only Percy's brilliant idea saved their lives.

Yes, Percy was sure he was bound to get himself in trouble. Well, there was no hope of changing things now. He was gone, and there was no way of bringing him back. Percy sighed as he sat on his bed and thought that maybe this was how his family in the

Outworld felt when they discovered he had run away from their cabin in Pan Woods. They didn't know where he had gone, if he were in trouble, or if he'd ever return. They didn't know he had, with the help of the mountain lion family, found his way into the underground kingdom known as the Aurora Dome. They probably also thought that if he were in trouble they wouldn't be able to help him. Yes, his family was probably feeling about him just as he felt about the Green Man. Unlike the Green Man, however, he had made an attempt to let his family know he was okay. He had come back to the cabin, and although they were gone he had left them a note saying he was okay and happy. He had even left them some valuable jewels. Still, he felt low and guilty when he thought about how he had run away.

He often thought he should go back, but he couldn't bring himself to do it. His family never seemed to love him. He didn't even look like his mother, father, or sister Beatrice. They were all tall with dark hair and eyes. He wasn't tall and had red hair, green eyes and freckles. He irritated his mother and sister, and his dad either ignored him or didn't know what to do with him. When he overheard his mother talking about taking him to doctors and putting him on medication, he decided to run away. What made it so hard to return to his Outworld family was the fact that he loved it here in the Aurora Dome. Everyone liked and admired him, and he was even someone special. He was actually the Champion of Aurora because he had saved everyone from an attack of the giant Basalt Beetles. King Priam and Queen Penelope considered him their closest adviser, and he and Princess Portia were best friends. No, he wouldn't go back, not just yet anyway.

Percy lay back on his bed. His eyes fluttered, and he nearly fell asleep. His arm fell to his side and he felt something hard. This startled him, and he sat up and looked at a book laying next to him. It was the volume of Aurora history that the Green Man had been reading just before he left. It interested their alien visitor because it talked about the adventures of Percy and Portia and mentioned a mysterious figure called Patecat. The Green Man thought this person might be his uncle. Percy was too tired to return it to the castle archives, so he heaved it onto his night stand and crawled under the covers.

While Percy is sleeping, this might be a good time to talk about "Uncle." Uncle and the Green Man come from a planet called Kolobro. They are called "Uncle" and the "Green Man" because their names in Kolobroian are such tongue twisters in English that it's best to call them by these names. The Green Man goes by that name because he wears a green skin-tight jump suit dimpled all over like a golf ball. On their planet technology is so advanced that it hardly exists at all any longer. You see, all their needs are met by devices called *Generatus*. They are commonly known as *Gens*, and there are only two models: the Transporter Gens, which are used exclusively for travel, and the MiniGens that are used for everything else. These MiniGens are used for making furniture, clothing, and all other objects, and for providing food.

Now Uncle spent most of his time traveling to other planets. He had traveled to so many that he got to the point where he only wanted to travel to unusual places, places where no Kolobroians had gone before. That's why he picked Earth for his destination. It was an out-of-the-way place that was suspected of being a boring, uninteresting planet.

He traveled to Earth about 500 years ago. (Kolobroians are a long-lived race, and 500 years on Earth is like a year on Kolobro.) He landed in Mexico and eventually got caught up in the war between the Spanish Conquistadors and the Aztecs. But that's another story. What's important here is the fact that Uncle got stranded on Earth. You might say he crash landed, and so he was unable to return to Kolobro. The Green Man came to Earth some 500 years later in order to find him.

Now, back to our story. In the underground kingdom of Aurora time is divided into three cycles. These are the active cycle, the quiet cycle, and the night or sleep cycle. There is no actual night in Aurora. The dome roof glows with the same white light all the time. Percy was awakened at the beginning of the active cycle by Portia. She was his alarm clock, because there were no clocks in Aurora, and he, being from the Outworld, didn't have that internal clock that told him when one cycle ended and another began.

"Percy, wake up!" she commanded. "I let you sleep longer than I should have, and we've got school!"

"I don't think I'll go this cycle," mumbled Percy.

"You have to go; we've missed enough as it is. Being with the Green Man took us away from school for cycles!"

"Okay, okay," yawned Percy. "I'm getting up."

"Don't be grumpy," urged Portia. "In natural history class Dr. Codexus is still talking about crystals, and you know how you like that. Hurry! I'll met you in the breakfast room."

She was gone before Percy could again complain about how much Dr. Codexus irritated him. (Dr. Codexus was not only a teacher at the Aurora school, but head librarian of Aurora. He disliked Percy as much as Percy disliked him. Dr. Codexus thought he was just a dumb boy who got lucky whenever an adventure came along.). Percy slipped out of bed, washed and put on his short, white robe with the gold spiral corkscrews on it. (Everyone in Aurora wore robes. Their color and symbols indicated their profession or position in the community. White with gold corkscrews meant you were nobility, so that's

6

what Princess wore. Percy, of course, wasn't of noble birth, but he wore the white with gold corkscrews too because he was the Champion of Aurora. The king and queen wore purple robes with gold corkscrews.)

King Priam and Queen Penelope had just finished eating when Percy arrived at the breakfast room. Portia was sitting next to her mother. They looked alike. Both were blonde and lovely, with large green eyes. The king looked more like Percy. He had short, unruly red hair, green eyes, but no freckles. The only other person in the room was Pouncer. That is, if you could call a mountain lion cub a person. (And you certainly could in Aurora. He and his father, Puma, and mother, Mom, were honored guests whenever they visited Aurora. That's because they were, and you'd already know this if you had read any of the other Percy Fitz books, the ones who first befriended Percy when he ran away, and whose cave leads to the Aurora Dome. Puma is also a prominent figure in all of Percy's other adventures.)

"You're late, Percy, my boy," said the king. "Both the fried fish and jade tea are cold. You'd better eat it anyway to keep up the old brain energy for school!"

"Yes, Percy. I understand there is a geometry test today," added the queen.

Percy mumbled something unintelligible and sat down. He hated geometry. He hated all kinds of math. Portia was good at it, but then she was good at everything. She was even good at sports! Percy admired her for being so smart. She was especially helpful when he didn't understand something at school.

"Where's Puma and Mom?" he asked as he gulped down the cold fish.

"They just left," whistled Pouncer. (Mountain lion language sounds like a series of soft whistles to a human, but once you understand it, it's every bit as good as English. Mountain lions can't speak English, but they can understand it.) "Mom said she'd had enough of Aurora and the Green Man," continued Pouncer. "She wanted to go back to the cave and the Outworld for a while. I wanted to stay, and King Priam said he'd hang out with me when you were in school. Besides, we never know when another adventure will happen, and I wanna be here for it!" His long tail whipped excitedly, and the hair in his black spots bristled.

Percy laughed. "Well, I hope it will be a long time before we have another adventure, if ever!"

"At least not dangerous adventures," said Portia. "A fun adventure wouldn't be bad."

"When have we ever had a fun adventure?" questioned Percy. "They all just about get us killed!"

"It's possible," declared Portia.

"Yeah," whistled Pouncer. "It's possible."

Pouncer was waiting outside the school when Percy and Portia got out. He always waited there whenever he could, not to greet his best friends, but to be made a great deal of by the other kids. They all stopped to pet him and comment on how handsome he is. (There are no normal animals in the Aurora Dome. The closest thing would be fish. All other animals are horrible creatures, like Manticoras, that have a body like a lion and a head like a man.)

Percy told Portia he thought he had passed the geometry test, but just barely. Portia suggested that before they studied for the natural history test, she should have him do some geometry problems, and that would tell her if he'd passed.

Pouncer began playing ball with some of the boys. "Pouncer," Percy called to him. "we're going to the right side castle tower to study. Meet us there when you're through playing ball."

Percy didn't usually like studying right after school, but he felt so uneasy about the test that he wanted to just to put his mind at ease. He had never failed a test, not even a trivium test, thanks to Portia, and he'd be very embarrassed if he'd flunked geometry. He had a reputation as somebody special, and he didn't want to disappoint people. He was the Champion of Aurora. And although he never felt like the champion of anything, he didn't want to let people down.

The Aurora castle has three corkscrew-shaped towers that are never used, except in an emergency, such as a Basalt Beetle attack, so Portia and Percy used the top of the right side one as their study hall. It was quiet, and there were no distractions. Most of the problems Percy was sure he answered correctly, but there were four he was fairly certain he got wrong. If he got all four wrong, he failed the test. If he got just one of them right, he passed. After going over them, Portia assured him he had gotten two right.

"Boy, that's a relief!" exclaimed Percy. "You know, one of my problems was I couldn't concentrate. I kept thinking about the Green Man. He's out there on a strange world, all by himself, and I keep wondering how he's going to keep himself out of trouble. How's he going to find his uncle. The Outworld is such a big place, and Uncle could be anywhere on it. He could have died or somehow found his way to another planet by now!"

"I know, I know, we should have gone with him," murmured Portia. "We just didn't think of it until it was too late.

"Yeah," agreed Percy. "You know he got in trouble to begin with by losing one of his

Transporter Gens. Maybe now he's on the surface of the earth and has lost one again. He'll be stuck without us. He won't be able to find his uncle, and won't be able to get back to his home planet."

"He said he'd been to twelve planets, but he had a planet pilot when he went to those," said Portia. "This was the first planet he'd been to on his own, and he botched it."

"Well, there's nothing we can do now, except hope everything goes all right."

"Hey, guys," whistled Pouncer, bounding into the room, "you still studying? Let's do something fun! Let's go to the lake and catch some fish!"

Pouncer always liked going fishing at Aurora Lake. He hardly ever caught anything, and Percy suspected going fishing was just an excuse of getting wet and playing in the water. Percy and Portia agreed, and so they went fishing. After fishing, there was a supper of boiled mushrooms, white worm noodles, and foaming flower mead. (Mushrooms grow abundantly in Aurora, and are not only a main source of food, but are used as a wood substitute and also to make clothes and paper, among other things.)

After supper, the king, queen, Portia, Percy and Pouncer went for a stroll in the Botanical Garden. Here is collected all the exotic mushrooms, flowers, and other plants that grow in the Aurora Dome.

"You and Percy are very quiet," observed Queen Penelope. "I imagine you've been thinking about the Green Man."

"Yes," said Portia. "We're worried about him. Even though he's a grown man, he's kind of like a little boy."

"He's hundreds of years old in Outworld time," said Percy, "but he doesn't look like he's over 30, and he does sometimes act like a little boy!"

"I wouldn't worry. He's made his way around

many worlds; he'll be okay on this one. He's probably already found his uncle, and they're off to someplace else," observed King Priam.

"I don't know, Your Majesty. I've got a feeling he's in trouble," said Percy uneasily.

"We should have gone with him, Dad," said Portia.

"Yeah," agreed Pouncer. "We should have gone with him and kept him out of trouble."

"Oh, I don't think so," trembled the queen. "He got you in terrible trouble the last time you went with him."

"Absolutely!" declared the king. "He's too great a bumbler. If you'd gone with him, we'd probably never have seen you again. He wouldn't be able to get you back here!"

When the night cycle began, and Percy returned to his room, he noticed the Aurora history volume still sitting on his night stand. Again he postponed returning it to the archives. He waited until the next quiet cycle and then ran to his room to retrieve it. It was then he noticed the strange object sticking out of the top, between the pages. It looked like some sort of bookmark at first, but when he pulled it out and examined it, it became obvious it was no ordinary bookmark. In fact, it was no bookmark at all.

It looked a little like a credit card, only it was longer and had no writing. It was thin, completely white, and its surface was finely ribbed on one side, giving it a corrugated or textured feeling. Percy could tell it wasn't made of plastic, like a credit card, but it also wasn't made of metal. Whatever it was made of, or whatever it was, it could have come from no one other than the Green Man! Percy ran to Portia's room to show her.

"It definitely was left by the Green Man," said Portia. "What do you think it is?" she asked, as she turned it over and over in her hand.

"I have no idea," declared Percy. "It sort of reminds me of what we call a credit card in the Outworld, but it's not one."

"Why did he leave it do you suppose?"

"You know him," replied Percy. "It's probably something he just forgot. I know I'm always putting things in books to mark my place -- you know, pens, scraps of paper, pebbles, whatever. He was probably marking his spot and forgot it was there. He forgets everything!"

"Yes, he does forget a lot, but I have a feeling he didn't forget this."

"What do you mean?"

"I mean," explained Portia, "I think he meant it for us."

"Well, if he meant it for us, why didn't he say so?" Percy asked. "And what are we supposed to do with it?"

Portia shrugged and handed the card back to him. They were sitting on the sofa in Portia's room, and

Percy held the card out in front of him. They both just silently stared at it. "Maybe it's a key," Percy finally said. "In the Outworld there are things like this that open doors."

"But what door would it open?" inquired Portia.

"Yeah, right. It couldn't be a key.

"Maybe it's just a bookmark after all," sighed Portia. "I mean, not a real bookmark; just something the Green Man used for one, but nothing meant for us."

Percy took it in both hands by his thumbs and forefingers. He rubbed his right thumb over the ribbed surface. The card vibrated and began to glow a bright white. The white dimmed to grey, and then after a few moments the Green Man's face filled the card.

Chapter 2

Is everyone insane in the Outworld?

"**P**ercy!" fumed the Green Man, "where have you been? I've been calling and calling and you never answered! And then the moment I'm not calling, you call me!"

Percy noted that a small picture of himself appeared in the upper right hand corner of the screen. He shifted the card, and a picture of Portia appeared next to him. "Oh, there you are too, Portia," exclaimed the Green Man. "Thank goodness I've contacted you both!"

"We didn't know you've been calling," explained Percy. "We only just found this card thing you left in the Aurora history book, and then it's only by accident we found out how to use it."

"What?! You mean I forgot to tell you about the Communication Slip? Well, come to think of it, I did forget to tell you about the Communication Slip! I remember now. I put it in the book when we were talking about the strange being it mentioned - - the one that I thought had to be Uncle. I was going to hand it to you just before I left. You know, as a way of contacting each other in case you needed me."

Portia shook her head slowly and looked at Percy. "It's a wonder we even found it!" she said. "We've been so worried about you. What's happening?"

"Plenty has happened!" exclaimed the Green Man. "I hardly know where to begin! I don't even know if I'm standing on my feet or standing on my head! I've got such a headache, I must be standing on my head!" Percy and Portia watched as he pressed his hand against his forehead and brushed aside the black curls. His handsome dark eyes were wide, and he looked dazed.

"Did you find Uncle?" Percy asked.

"Yes, yes, that's where I should begin! Yes, I found Uncle. It was really quite easy once I got out from beneath the Earth. I think the Earth's magnetic resonance was blocking the signal. And, well, never mind that. The short of it is I got a weak signal from his MiniGen, and I was able to follow that." He smiled broadly, showing his perfect white teeth.

"So, what's wrong?" asked Portia. "Aren't you happy you found him?"

"Of course I'm happy I found him, but, but, I hardly know how to explain! I've been to twelve worlds, but never to one where the entire population is insane! First of all, everyone's dressed strangely, like they're all from different planets. Yet I know this planet has no interplanetary travel. Then there's this guy taking notes and photos; and then there're two people who act like they want to arrest everybody. But

16

the worst thing is, Uncle won't leave! He says he likes it here, but I'm not sure he does. Then he says he can't leave right now in any case. Then there's this other man who hangs around him all the time, and I think he may have some strange hold over Uncle. And then we're in this huge building, and hardly anybody seems to leave it, and more and more people are coming into it!" The Green Man stopped talking and took a deep breath.

"I'm afraid you're not making much sense," said Portia, as kindly as she could.

"I'm not? Well, I suppose I'm not, but it's because this place is crazy, and it's making me crazy, too! Say, maybe that's it! Maybe I'm in an insane asylum. You know, a place where they keep crazy people! Maybe Uncle is a patient, maybe even an inmate! That's it. They've got him drugged, and that's why he doesn't want to leave!"

"Calm down," said Percy. "Is there any sign or something that has the name of the place on it?"

"Outside the door there's a sign that says 'Desert Wind Hotel and Convention Center'."

"What city is that in?" Percy asked.

"I don't know, but I don't believe it's any great distance from the Outworld above the Aurora Dome. You see, after I left there, I landed on a mountaintop just above you. That was a fortunate thing because it was a good vantage point to scan the entire hemisphere for any sign of Uncle. As luck would have

17

it, I picked up a weak signal and followed it to this place."

"It's wonderful that you've found him," said Portia. "I'm proud of you."

Another broad smile spread across the Green Man's face. "It was pretty brilliant of me, wasn't it! I mean, I got the coordinates just right, and nothing went wrong."

"Yes," Portia agreed. "But now what can we do to help you?"

"You and Percy have to come here and help me sort things out. I don't know what to do. I feel completely helpless. Uncle was glad to see me, and we had a brief talk. I told him the entire family was worried about him, and so I had come to search him out. First of all, he explained that he had been stranded here. When he landed on Earth, he lost not one but both his Transporter Gens! Imagine that, him, an expert transporter pilot losing both his Transporter Gens! It doesn't make me look so bad, losing just one of mine, does it? So there was no way he could get back to Kolobro. He had only one MiniGen and so."

"Right," interrupted Percy, "but to get back to your problem, how can we help, and if we're going to help, how do we get to where you are?"

"I'll come get you. I left the Communication Slip there just in case I needed you. And if I didn't, at least I'd let you know if I found Uncle. But as things turned out, I'm going to need your help in this crazy place right away! I mean I need to understand what's going on here, and what Uncle is up to." He mopped his face with a large white cloth that looked like a pillow case.

"We'll have to get permission from Mom and Dad," said Portia, "but I think there should be no problem."

"You're sure you can make it here and back there again with no problem?" asked Percy, still uneasy about the Green Man's skill. "I mean, there's no chance that you will lose a Transporter Gen or anything?"

"What? You think I might bungle things?" The Green Man looked shocked and surprised, as if he had forgotten the problems he'd had just days ago. "No, no," he assured them, "there won't be any problems. The coordinates are all set in the Gens, and since I'm not transporting to another planet, there's no possibility of losing anything. Can I come right now?"

"Let us call you back,' advised Portia.

"Okay, but don't take too long." The Green Man nodded, and they saw his thumb appear on the screen. The screen immediately turned white. Percy rubbed his thumb across his screen, and it turned white as well.

"I know I told the Green Man there wouldn't be a problem, but I don't think Mom and Dad are going to let us go," murmured Portia. "I mean, we just got back from The Rings, and they know how dangerous that was. And the Green Man is not the most reliable

19

person we know. They're not going to like us going with him again."

"You're right," agreed Percy, "but do you think we shouldn't go with him? "

"No, I think we should go. I want to go, but I am a little worried about getting back. I just have this feeling that something will go wrong, and he won't be able to bring us back. I've been to the Outworld twice, and it's so big, so huge, I'm just afraid that if we're not transported back, we'd never be able to find the way by ourselves. I mean, his uncle is stranded, and he's an expert planet pilot. I know the Green Man said there's no possibility, but you know him. What if we were stranded?"

Percy put his arm around her shoulder. "You don't have to worry about that. He said that he wasn't far from Aurora, which means he's probably in the United States. If for some reason he couldn't bring us back, I could find our way back. I know how to find my way to Pan Woods from anyplace in the U.S. And we both know how to find our way from Pan Woods to the mountain lion cave, and from the mountain lion cave down through the tunnels to Aurora!"

"That makes me feel much better. You have to realize that to someone like me that has spent her whole life in the Netherworld, the Outworld is a little scary."

"Yeah, I can understand that," agreed Percy. "But now, to get back to your parents. . ."

"Hey, I just thought of another problem! It's you! Last time we were in the Outworld people everywhere were looking for you. You were the lost boy with posters of you in all the stores, and your picture was on T.V. You're the kid everyone wants to find! What are we going to do about that?"

"I forget about that," admitted Percy. "It has been months since I ran away. At least I think it's been months, so people probably aren't looking for me anymore. And we won't be traveling in a motor home and stopping where people might recognize me like we did the first time."

"That's right," agreed Portia. "We'll travel in the transporter room and go directly to that building where Uncle is."

"Yeah, and if I just stay in the building with you and the Green Man, probably nobody will even think I'm a runaway. We probably don't have to worry about that!"

"That building sounds kind of weird, with people going in but not going out. Do you think there's any danger there?" asked Portia.

Percy laughed. "I think I know what that building is. It's some big hotel. It's where people stay when they're traveling far away from home. The Green Man probably saw a lot of people checking in."

"What about the strange way they were dressed? Do people who travel far away from home dress funny?"

21

"I'm not sure what that's all about," admitted Percy. "Let's downplay that part when we talk to your parents."

Chapter 3

A stowaway!

Portia and Percy found King Priam and Queen Penelope in the throne room listening to a dispute between two fishermen. It seems their nets had become entangled, and one of the fishermen, rather than patiently untangling them, had pulled them both into his boat and then cut the others net in order to release his. The offending fisherman complained to the king and queen that this was the second time this had happened, and he was tired of it!

The king and queen consulted in whispers. "You," said the king, pointing at the net cutter, "must learn to be patient, as all fishermen should be. You must buy a new net for Peter here. Peter, in future you will take special care not to tangle your net in the net of others! The two fishermen bowed their heads as a sign of agreement and, without another word, left the throne room.

"Now," said King Priam with a smile, "what dispute can we settle between you two?"

"I don't know," murmured Queen Penelope, laughing softly, "they look pretty serious. All our wisdom may be needed to settle this one."

Percy decided to let Portia do the talking. As they walked forward, he let her go first. She stepped onto her father's throne and sat on his lap.

"Oh, dear," Queen Penelope said. "I don't like the looks of this!"

"Nor do I," agreed the king. "Whenever she sits on my lap, she wants something she shouldn't have!"

Portia kissed him on the forehead. "Can't I just sit on your lap because I love you?"

"No," protested the king, "you can't. You want something. You got this artifice from your mother. She used to do the same thing!"

"Priam," exclaimed the queen. "I did no such thing!"

"You did, my sweet, you did, and always got what you asked for!"

"Is there something you wanted, my dear," asked Queen Penelope, ignoring her husband.

"We just heard from the Green Man," said the princess. "Percy discovered a communication device he left behind."

Percy held up the Communication Slip. Upon hearing Portia and seeing this, the king stood up so quickly that Portia slid from his lap and landed with a thump on the floor. "You've heard from that, that crazy man!" exclaimed the king. "No doubt he wants you two to do something. Am I right? He's got himself in a stew, and he wants you to rescue him!"

"Now, Priam, calm down. Let's hear what they

have to say before we get upset," advised the queen.

"Okay, okay," gulped the king. "We'll hear what they have to say, and then I'll say NO! They were nearly frozen to death in The Rings the last time they helped him!" He ran both hands through his red hair, standing it on end.

"He left this device just so he could let us know when he found his uncle. The only thing is, he forgot to tell us, and we never would have known if I hadn't found it in a book," explained Percy.

"Yes," continued Portia. "Percy figured out how to use it, and immediately a picture of the Green Man appeared on it, and . . ."

"And he is in trouble, right?" roared King Priam. "He's always in trouble!"

"Well yes," said Percy. "He's sort of in trouble."

"Not bad trouble, not dangerous trouble," interjected Portia.

"No," said Percy, "not dangerous trouble. It's just that he's found Uncle but needs some help coping with the Outworld."

"He's been to other planets, you see," explained Portia, "but never to one like Earth, and he doesn't know quite what to do."

"I know what he can do," roared the king. "He can get himself out of whatever it is!"

"Priam, calm down, my dear. Let the children finish explaining," soothed Queen Penelope.

Percy then proceeded to relate all that the Green

Man had said over the Communication Slip. He ended by saying, "I think he's in a hotel -- that's a place where people stay when they travel a long way from their homes. It's a perfectly safe place. The people who run hotels are always nice, and I can't imagine there could be any danger."

"What about all the people that are dressed strangely?" asked Queen Penelope.

"Well, that is a puzzle," admitted Percy. "But he didn't say anything about them being dangerous. I think there must be some simple explanation"

"And so he wants to come here and get the two of you and take you to this hotel place?" asked the king. "And he assures you, for whatever good that is, that there's no danger in using that disappearing room of his?"

"He said that the coordinates were all set, and there wouldn't be any problem," Portia replied.

"I'm not too worried about that," observed Percy. "Once the settings are made, there shouldn't be any problem, and once we're there, there's no chance we won't be back. As I was telling Portia, once we're at the hotel, if something goes wrong, I can always find our way back to Aurora, even without the Green Man."

"What about school?" asked the queen. "You've already missed a lot with all of Percy's adventures."

"We shouldn't be gone long," assured Percy, always glad to get away from school.

"We're caught up on all our homework," Portia added.

"Portia, you and Percy take a walk while your father and I talk this over," Queen Penelope said.

They left the throne room and were walking down the hall toward the front of the castle when they met Pouncer. He was sliding on his back toward them. This was one of his favorite tricks. He would run along the polished stone floor, then flip on his back and slide down the hall, spinning like a pinwheel.

"Hey, hi guys," he whistled, bumping up against Percy. "I was wondering where you were. What's up? You two look way serious."

Percy explained what had happened. The more he talked, the more the hair on Pouncer's neck stood on end. "So you think we might be going on another adventure?" whistled Pouncer.

"Not *we*," said Portia gently. "Just Percy and me. We couldn't take you without your parents' permission."

"I could go get 'em," suggested Pouncer.

"No, that would take too long," said Percy. "Besides, you couldn't go anyway. We can't take mountain lions into a hotel. They're not allowed. You know what would happen if you were with a whole bunch of humans!"

"But I want to go!" whined Pouncer. "I've only gotten to go on one of your adventures! I missed all the rest!"

27

"You can go on the next one," assured Portia.

Just then a servant found them and said the king and queen wished to see them in the throne room.

"We've talked it over," Queen Penelope said, "and decided that you can go. I'll talk to Dr. Codexus and get any assignments you will miss at school. I expect you both to make them up promptly when you return."

"I don't think we will be gone long enough to miss much," said Percy.

"There are two more conditions," interrupted King Priam. "First, you must take the Oculus with you. That will help you foresee danger, should there be any. Second, you leave that communication thing with us so we can keep in contact with you should the need arise. If you won't do those two things, you can't go!" The king then stared up at the ceiling and ran both hands through his hair.

"Agreed!" cried Portia and Percy in unison.

Before the Green Man was called, the Oculus was retrieved from its special box. (For those of you who have refused to read the other Percy Fitz books, the Oculus is an eyeball attached to an ornate silver bracelet. It is housed in a box filled with a clear, jelly-like liquid. When the bracelet is placed on a person's wrist, it somehow connects with that person's brain. That person can then do two things. He can command the eyeball, known as the Oculus, to leave the bracelet and fly to any location, and he can also see in his head what the Oculus sees. One other important thing to know about the Oculus is that it doesn't work with everyone. Nobody knows why. But it does work with Percy.)

Percy placed the Oculus, still dripping with goo, on his left arm. He felt a sudden sensation of dizziness, but that immediately passed. The king then gave both Portia and Percy a small mushroom leather pouch filled with pea-sized gold nuggets. "For emergencies," he explained.

"What about clothes," exclaimed Portia. "We'll need some Outworld clothes. I've still got my shorts and shirt from last time!"

"Let's wait on that," suggested Percy. "Let's see what the Green Man thinks we should wear. He did say everybody was dressed weird. He can always zap up some new clothes with his MiniGen ."

"Okay, then, I guess we're ready," said Portia.

"Wait a minute," declared King Priam. "You haven't shown us how to use that communication thing!"

"Oh, yeah," said Percy. He handed it to the king, who immediately handed it to Queen Penelope, saying, "You'd better handle this."

"Hold it in your hand," instructed Percy, "with the rough side facing you, and rub your thumb up and down on it."

The Communication Slip flickered, and the white surface turned light grey. About a minute passed

29

before the Green Man's face appeared on the screen. "What!? What!" exclaimed the Green Man. "Oh, yes, it's you, Queen Penelope. I was surprised to see a face other than Percy or Portia's. I hope you haven't bad news for me. I've already had bad news. Uncle refuses to even see me, let alone talk to me, for the next three days! He says he's too busy right now, and that I wouldn't understand how things are. He says that when this is over, he'll try to explain. I don't even know what he means by *things*! Is that Percy there behind you?"

"Yes, I'll let him speak with you, but first King Priam and I want to get your assurance that if we allow Portia and Percy to go with you, they will be in no danger."

"Danger? No, no, they will be in no danger. The only danger would be if they went crazy like the rest of the people in this place, and I don't really think crazy is contagious. I've been to twelve worlds, your Highness, and I've never seen anything like this. There's hardly anybody here that's normal. Of course, what's normal on one planet isn't necessarily normal on another. For example, on planet 6667 they slap your face to show they like you. But what I've experienced here goes beyond all reason! And now that Uncle won't speak to me, I'm in more of a quandary than ever as to what to do."

"And you think Portia and Percy can help?" asked King Priam, peering over the queen's left shoulder.

30

"I don't know who else possibly could!" sighed the Green Man, wiping his forehead with what looked like a pillowcase. "Percy's had experience in the Outworld, and Portia is so sensible and levelheaded, they're the only ones I can turn to."

"And you're not going to get them lost or encased inside a stone wall or anything?" asked King Priam.

"No, no, no, there's no chance of that," assured the Green Man. "All the transporter settings are locked in place and won't be changed!"

"All right," grumbled the king, "they can go, but if anything happens, I'm sending my whole army to find them and you! And when I do find them, and I will, you're going to the castle dungeon for a long stay!'

Before the king could say any more, Queen Penelope quickly handed the Communication Slip to Percy. "I say, Percy, tell the king he needn't worry. Nothing will go wrong, and I'll have the two of you back in no more than four or five Outworld days. I hope. I'll be transporting in a few minutes, and I'll land in the castle courtyard, just where I left."

Before Percy could say anything, the screen turned blank and the Green Man was gone. Everyone stood there silently looking at one another. Finally the queen suggested that they should take some food, but Percy said they wouldn't need any. Portia suggested her sunglasses, and Percy agreed with that, but thought that the Green Man could really provide anything they needed, probably even money. Portia liked the sunglasses she had bought in the adventure of the Dome of Doom, and so she went to her room for those. The only thing Percy wanted was his Leatherman Multi-tool, and he always had that in the pocket of his robe.

(It is a curious thing to note, but it should be noted here, that as soon as the Green Man had hung up the Communication Slip, Pouncer slipped quietly and unnoticed out of the room.)

Portia came back wearing the sunglasses that made her look like some famous movie star.

"Well, we'd better go to the courtyard," she said. "The Green Man may already be there."

When they arrived at the courtyard, the Green Man wasn't there, and no one noticed that Pouncer wasn't with them. He had been completely forgotten in the excitement of the moment. He was there, however. He was hiding along the side of the steps and quietly watching and waiting.

With a loud pop and a bright white glow, the transporter room suddenly appeared before them. It was about the size of Percy's bedroom, and its almost invisible walls and ceiling could just barely be seen as a slight quivering in the air, rather like heat waves rippling off a hot highway. The Green Man and a table were about the only things in it. He pressed the button on the MiniGen in his hand, and in an instant the rippling walls disappeared and the room was gone. The table remained. On it was a Transporter Gen, and another one lay tilted at an angle on the ground, four feet from the table.

"Boy, am I glad to see you," he sighed, as he stepped toward them. "Not only that, but I'm glad to be in a place where no one's crazy!" Without the least ceremony he hugged Portia and then Percy. He then made a low bow to the king and kissed Queen Penelope's hand. The king ran his hands through his hair when the queen's hand was kissed, and only made the slightest nod of the head when he was bowed to.

"Now, you're sure that your transporter is safe and there's no danger at this hotel place?" were the first words out of the king's mouth.

"Quite safe and quite sure," replied the Green Man. "It's just as I said before. Everyone appears to suffer from some form of insanity. There's lots of activity with more people coming than going. Some people are dressed normally, while others are dressed outlandishly. Some are even dressed as what I would call non-humans and aliens! I have developed a theory however. I suspect that maybe they're all not crazy; maybe there's some sort of insurrection or rebellion afoot." The king and queen both raised their eyebrows.

"Not a violent sort of rebellion, no, no," assured the Green Man, noting their alarm. "No, it's more of a 'I'm not going to be like everyone else' rebellion. You know, like when a kid wears a muffin on his head and says he's a turtle." The eyebrows raised on both the king and queen, and they gazed at one another. They were about to say something when the Green Man continued. "No, no, it can't be that. They are probably just ordinary lunatics like you find everywhere." A frown spread across the Green Man's face. "But then, maybe it's both rebellion and lunacy."

While this was going on, a small, tan figure with black spots and four legs was silently sneaking toward the Green Man's table. Once under it, it crouched down, making itself as small and unnoticeable as possible.

"What about you, Percy?" asked Queen Penelope, her uneasiness expressed on her face. "Does this sound safe to you?"

"I think so," said Percy. "I'm beginning to have an idea about what's going on. I'll have to go there to be sure, but if it's what I'm thinking, there's no danger at all."

"Very well," growled the king. "It's time you were off. The sooner gone, the sooner you'll return to us."

The three walked toward the table. The Green Man pointed his MiniGen at the Transporter Gen on the table, and the room walls enclosed and wavered around them.

"Wait a minute. What about our clothes?" recalled Percy. "Do we need to change clothes, or will you zap us up different clothes when we get there?"

"Are you kidding?" chuckled the Green Man. "You'll fit right in with what you're wearing! You'll be just two more weirdos!"

The king was about to object to that comment when the Green Man again pointed his MiniGen at the Transporter Gen on the table and pushed the button. There was a loud pop and a bright white light, and they disappeared from Aurora.

Chapter 4

What's a UFO convention?

They landed, or more accurately reappeared in the far end of a half-empty parking lot. It was night, and parking lot lights glared down upon them. The Green Man pushed the button on his MiniGen, and the transporter room and this time the table as well disappeared. All that remained on the pavement were two Transporter Gens and a brown spotted fur ball that unrolled itself to reveal none other than Pouncer!

"Pouncer!" Portia and Percy exclaimed in unison.

"What! What?" gasped the Green Man.

"What are you doing here?" demanded Percy. "I told you you couldn't go with us! You'll ruin everything! Once people see you, you'll be hauled off to an animal shelter or a zoo! You know you can't go among people in the Outworld!"

"Well, I didn't want to miss out on an adventure!" pouted Pouncer. "I forgot about being around other people."

"We'll have to take him back!" declared Percy.

The Green Man smiled and raised an eyebrow. "Maybe not. Maybe it would be a good idea to keep him with us."

"Trust me, it won't be a good idea," fumed Percy. "Outworld people don't like mountain lions wandering around their hotels, not even cub mountain lions!"

"Ah, but I've already seen four cats wandering around this hotel, and they weren't much smaller than Pouncer. The only difference was that they had silver leashes on them. All we need is a silver leash on Pouncer!"

"Well, that's weird," declared Percy. "I haven't been in a lot of hotels, but the ones I've been in never allowed animals, but whatever you say!"

The Green Man took a MiniGen out of his shoulder bag, did some adjustments to it, and pressed the button. There was a soft pop and a flash, and a silver leash and collar appeared on the ground. "Portia, put that on him," he said. "And it would probably be best if you were in charge of him and held the leash. The cats I saw had girls holding the leashes."

"And you'd better do everything we say, or I'll send you to the animal shelter!" threatened Percy.

A hot, dry breeze enveloped them. It was as if an oven door had been opened in their faces.

Percy looked at the building at the other end of the parking lot. There was a covered walkway that led up to a double door. Above the walkway a neon sign read "Desert Wind Hotel and Convention Center."

"It is hot!" cried Portia. "This can't be the right

place, can it Percy? There can't be anyplace in the Outworld this hot!"

"Oh, it's the right place," said the Green Man, as he put the two Transporter Gens in the shoulder bag. (It never seemed to get any fatter no matter how much stuff he put in it!) "I told you I had the coordinates right and there would be no trouble!" He displayed one of his winning grins.

"It can sometimes get even hotter than this in the Outworld." Percy said. "I think we must be somewhere in Arizona, or maybe in Las Vegas. It gets really hot in those places."

"I never bothered to ask where this place is," sighed the Green Man. "Uncle probably wouldn't have told me if I'd asked. I don't know what's happened to him. He was always jolly and friendly to me. Now he tells me not to bother him and to stay out of his way. Let's go in."

"Are you sure our clothes are okay?" asked Portia, very uneasy at appearing in the Outworld in her Aurora robe.

"Yeah, your green jumpsuit is covered by nice slacks and a green golf shirt," Percy said. "How come you changed out of your green suit, but we should stay dressed in these Aurora robes. I feel kind of dumb!" (It should be noted that all the time Percy and Portia had known the Green Man, he had always been dressed in a skintight green jumpsuit with golf ball-like dimples all over it. This suit covered everything but his feet, hands, and head.)

" Well, I wanted to dress like Uncle, but I have a feeling that you'll fit in better if you stay dressed the way you are."

They walked through the double door of the hotel and down a short hallway. It opened into a large area with a long registration desk. A number of overstuffed chairs and couches were scattered about. Against the wall, opposite the hotel registration desk, were three folding tables covered with cloth. Fastened to the wall above these was a sign that read "Tenth Annual Southwest Region UFO Convention." Below that in capital letters was the word "WELCOME." Behind the tables sat three individuals, and on the tables were piles of folders and signs that read "Registration."

Gathered around these registration tables were a strangely dressed collection of people. There were men, women and young people dressed in gold and silver spacesuits. Others were dressed in blue jumpsuits with what appeared to be wings painted on their backs. Some were dressed as strange creatures with four arms and dragon-like headdresses. Still others were dressed like robots. Many were dressed in white or light-grey bodysuits and wore helmets with large black eyes and very small mouths and noses. To Percy and Portia the most shocking of all costumes were the ones that looked almost exactly like their clothes! Wearing these were young people dressed in short white robes. The girls had long blonde hair and

39

the boys short blonde hair. The robes were plain white, however, without the gold spiral corkscrews that Portia and Percy had. One couple even had a larger yellow house cat on a silver leash. Its ears and tail were dyed black.

"It's just about what I thought." said Percy. "When you described all the people as dressing strangely, I thought it might be a science fiction convention. I was close; it's a UFO convention! People don't always dress funny when they go to hotels. It's just when they go to hotels where they're having these kinds of conventions that they dress up. I went to a science fiction convention with my cousin for one afternoon last year. It looked a lot like this."

"I have a few questions," whispered Portia, pulling at Percy's sleeve. "What is a convention, what is a UFO, and why are some people dressed like us?"

"Yeah, and why is that kitty cat on a silver rope like me?" whistled Pouncer.

"A convention," explained Percy, "is where a bunch of people who like the same things get together to talk about it, dress in costumes, and enjoy being with one another. They also attend lectures telling about new information in their field of interest."

(The Green Man was listening to this as closely as Portia, for he had no idea what a convention or UFO was either.)

"A UFO,' continued Percy, "is an unidentified flying object. It means a spaceship that has come to earth from some other planet. UFO also includes the people or creatures that have come in the spaceship. You remember, Portia, how Rufus McGee was telling us about the UFO he saw in the sky outside his cabin one night? It's kind of like that. Some people believe there are spaceships and creatures from other planets, and some people don't. There has never been any real proof."

"Haw!" scoffed the Green Man. "Little do they know that there are plenty of 'creatures,' as you call us, from other planets. And some of us visit this nowhere planet called Earth! But some of us are from more advanced worlds that don't use low-tech spaceships to get here!"

"But what about the people dressed like us?" said Portia.

"I have no idea," murmured Percy.

"A mystery that Uncle could solve if he'd talk to me," grumbled the Green Man, "but now you know why I had you keep your regular clothes on. You blend right in!"

"That part is really weird," said Percy, shaking his head. "Do you suppose there are others from the Netherworld here, too?"

"I don't think so. They don't look quite right somehow. They look like Outworlders dressed up like me," observed Portia. She turned to the Green Man. "You don't suppose there are people on other planets that look like us, do you?"

The Green Man shrugged. "Who knows. I've only been to twelve worlds. Some of our scientists say that for every world that exists, there's another just exactly like it."

"Well, what should we do now?" asked Percy. "Should we get some rooms, or register for the convention or what? You don't think we could go right now to see Uncle, do you?"

"Yes, well, I'd like to go see Uncle, but I don't think he would see me. He said not to bother him, but maybe with you three along he'd talk to us. Percy, I'm sure you could find out what's going on."

They all got on an elevator, got off on the 10th floor, and walked to the end of the hall. The Green Man knocked at room 1011. The door opened a few inches, and one eye and a nose appeared. "Not now, Pizflicofimacax," a voice said, but before anymore words could escape, Pouncer pushed his way into the room, pulling Portia with him and knocking Uncle backwards. Percy and the Green Man quickly followed. (Pizflicofimacax is the Green Man's real name. Now you can understand why Portia and Percy call him the Green Man.)

The room was a large one, furnished with two couches, two recliners, a long table with chairs around it, and a big screen T.V. The man who answered looked like the Green Man. His hair was black and wavy; he wasn't quite as tall as the Green Man, but was as thin. He definitely looked older, and his eyes were brown instead of black like his nephew's.

"What's all this?" demanded Uncle. "Never mind, don't say anything. Look, you're a good boy, Pizflicofimacax, and I'm glad you're here, and I'm happy to see you, but you've come at a terrible time. I just can't deal with you and all that's going on right now. I have to give our work and troubles my full attention. Look, you can stay here with me; there's plenty of room; but just don't bother me for the next three days."

"But, but I brought some friends. They're really smart, and they may be able to help."

Across the room, seated at the table, was an older man with a bald head and a huge, grey mustache. "What's all this about, Adam?" he grumbled. "We've got to concentrate on figuring this all out. We may not even break even on this one, and if that Tono woman finds out anything, we may be done for good! Who is this fellow and his children, anyway?" He slammed a clipboard on the table and pushed his chair back.

"Don't you remember, Barney, we met my nephew in the lobby. This is him, but I don't know his friends here."

"Yes, I remember, but I didn't pay much attention. I was on my way up here; and, besides, I didn't think he was your *real* nephew. I just assumed he was a young friend you'd met at another convention."

"I *am* his real nephew," said the Green Man, "and

43

this is Princess Portia and Percy Fitz, and this little fellow here is Pouncer. He's a mountain lion cub."

Barney stood up and came over to the companions. He eyed them curiously. "Now wait a minute here! This is your real nephew, and these are his friends, and this one is a princess? That means that at least two of them are not from *here*, right? That means that two of them are like you, right? Great walloping walruses! This makes things even worse! Make them go away; send them somewhere else. They can't stay here. They can't even stay in Phoenix! We have too many of their kind here already!"

Barney began pacing the floor. Percy thought that if this old fellow were to lay on his belly, he'd look remarkably like a walloping walrus. He wasn't sure, however, what a walrus did when it walloped.

All of the companions, even Pouncer wondered who this Barney was and what he was talking about. "Well now, I'm even more confused," the Green Man confessed. "First of all you tell me you are stranded on this planet and won't leave. Now it looks like this Barney fellow knows all about you, and you seem to be involved with him in something sinister! Has he got some hold over you? What are you two doing, and why is he so anxious for us to leave? And why won't you talk to me for three or four days?"

Uncle took the Green Man by the arm and led him to one of the couches. "Sit down, my boy. Sit down, Barney, and the rest of you. I guess we'll just have to take the time to explain everything. I don't know what good it will do, and I don't see how you or your friends can help, but who knows."

Chapter 5

Uncle's story

"As you know, nephew, I've traveled to many worlds. In fact, so many worlds that I lost count of how many. World traveling was my passion and only interest. Then one day I decided to travel to this planet, Earth. It was on our star charts, and somebody had traveled here in the dim past. They had noted that it was a very ordinary, uninteresting planet, with nothing to recommend it. Now since I had been to so many extraordinary, fascinating, and fabulous planets in the galaxy, I was interested in traveling someplace different. Oh, there were other planets on the star chart considered uninteresting, but for some unaccountable reason Earth intrigued me." Uncle began pacing around the table, taking long strides and looking full of pent-up energy and emotion. The emotion was most likely worry.

"So I calibrated my Transporter Gens and traveled here. Well, things went wrong almost immediately. Went wrong for me, a master planet pilot! You know how when you transport there is a bright light and a popping sound, and then you feel a bit dizzy, and electricity seems to course and tingle through your body, and then, pop, you're where you are going? Well, everything started out as normal until I got to the tingling part, then I felt as if somebody had thrown me inside a large metal barrel and was shaking it! I was banged and thumped and rolled about until I thought I was going to be turned to jelly!" Uncle wiped his brow with the back of his hand.

"Then there was a clanging sound, and no pop, and I found my transporter room had crashed in a jungle. Both my Transporter Gens were gone. I don't know how, but I suspect they somehow vaporized on entering the Earth's atmosphere.

"When I came to my senses and got my bearings, I discovered I was on the outskirts of a city that we now call Mexico City. The natives, who were Aztecs, came flocking around me. Some of them were warriors with shields and spears. They were very ferocious and were jabbering at me in a threatening manner. Of course, I wasn't worried because I was still inside the transporter room, and so they couldn't hurt me. Finally, a young warrior, not much older than your friend, Percy, threw a spear at me. It bounced off the transporter room, and did that cause a sensation! Several other spears were then thrown, then sticks were poked, and, finally, hands began feeling the invisible walls.

"I was perfectly safe and comfortable and decided to just wait and see what would happen. Never in my travels had I encountered such a primitive culture. My only concern was the loss of my Transporter Gens. At that point, I was pretty certain that if they hadn't vaporized, they had just somehow fallen out of the room when I crash-landed; and that I would be able to find them somewhere nearby lying on the jungle floor. It was only later that I determined they were nowhere on Earth.

"So using my MiniGen I conjured up an easy chair and ate meat pie with gravy and waited for what would happen next. A great crowd gathered all around me, and then a path was made through it; and who should appear but a man I found out later was the great king Montezuma himself! Great plumes of white and green feathers flowed out of his headdress, and his long cape was made of thousands of smaller red, green, and yellow feathers. Around his waist was an ornate gold belt that must have weighed fifty pounds! He began talking to me in a very loud and commanding voice. Of course, at that point I hadn't been able to connect with his mind to download his language into my mind, so I didn't know what he was saying.

"Then he and all the others dropped to their knees and raised their hands above their heads. I realized immediately that they thought I was some god. Well, not to belabor the story too long, King Montezuma and I became good friends after I downloaded his language, and I soon let him know that I wasn't a god, but a traveler from another planet. He wouldn't accept

48

this, and so to save a lot of time and argument, I agreed to be a minor god who had come just to visit the Aztec people."

"But you still had your MiniGens?" interrupted Percy. "When the Aztecs saw you use those, that would convinced them you were a god."

"Well, first of all, I only had one. Being an experienced traveler and a master planet pilot, I never found the need for more than one. And, yes, the MiniGen did astound and frighten them, but I tried to use it sparingly and only for basic things, mainly for my own comfort."

"But didn't you also use it to help the people?" asked Portia. "I would think there were many good things you could have done for them."

"I didn't; not at first anyway. You see, we have a law on Kolobro, our home planet that travelers are not allowed to interfere with the politics, cultures, and technologies of other planets. So I did do some things that I felt wouldn't break the law, such as heal some sick children, and provide extra food for the poor, but nothing I thought was major. Then the Spanish invaders came and everything changed."

"So you were there when Cortez and his men came!" exclaimed Percy. "And so, did you fight with the Aztecs? With you on their side, they should have won the war!"

"Yes, I was there, but since I had to obey the laws of Kolobro, I couldn't interfere. When Montezuma realized that the Aztec Empire was going to be destroyed, he asked me to take a group of his people, along with some of the Aztec records and treasure, to the lands north, where the people, records, and treasure would be safe. I decided I had to do that even if it meant bending the law a little bit."

"We know some of what happened after that," exclaimed Percy, " because Portia and I have been to Aztlan!"

Uncle's jaw dropped open in surprise. "You have! So it still exists? Do Aztecs still live there? How could you possibly have been there?"

"Yes, it still exits, and, yes, Aztecs still live there, but how we got there is a story for another time," said Percy.

"That's right," agreed Portia, anxious to hear the rest of Uncle's story so that she and Percy could figure out how to help him. "Please, go on with your story."

"Several small groups of us, at different times, took the ancient trails north to look for a hiding place. I was the leader of the first group. I finally found a spot in the desert of what is now known as Central Utah. There was a large mound, and hidden in the side of the mound was a cave. Not to go into a lot of detail, that cave wasn't very deep, and so I used my MiniGen to carve it deeper into the earth until we eventually broke through to a natural tunnel that lead to a large natural cavern containing light, water, and even a jungle. The Aztecs named it Aztlan.

50

"We hid the treasure and sacred records in the caves between the desert and Aztlan, and, using my knowledge and the MiniGen, we built a city and temple there. Then disaster struck. The river flowing around the city rose. It rose quickly and unexpectedly and flooded the tunnel leading to the treasure and the surface of the earth. We thought the water would eventually recede, but it never did."

"Couldn't you cut a new tunnel to the surface with your MiniGen?" asked Percy.

"I could have," agreed Uncle, "but then another disaster happened. The temple was about finished, and I was using the MiniGen to lift and transport stone blocks to the top of the temple pyramid when the MiniGen started to overheat."

"What do you mean overheat?" exclaimed the Green Man. "MiniGens never overheat. They're always cool to the touch, no matter what they're doing. You can't even get a MiniGen hot if you throw it into a fire!"

"I know," agreed Uncle, "but my MiniGen got hot! So hot it cracked. The stone I was lifting tumbled down the side of the pyramid, and the MiniGen never worked right thereafter!

I could perform small, uncomplicated tasks with it, but it would never lift a stone or slice through rock again. I could adjust it to make simple foods, like bread, or popcorn, but pot roast or ice cream were out of the question. I could conjure a blanket, but not a chair. And over the years the thing has grown weaker and weaker. Now all it will do is very simple things like moving a ball across a table or lifting a sheet of paper into the air."

"So, when that happened you really were stranded in Aztlan and on Earth," observed Portia.

"Exactly," continued Uncle. "I made the best of it, however. After several more years in Aztlan, I got the idea to build a submarine and see if I could find my way back to the surface of the Earth following the river currents. So I worked with the materials at hand and built what the Aztecs called the Itzcoatal."

"So, you're the one who invented the Itzcoatal! Portia and I, we used it to escape Aztlan in the adventure of the Measureless Cavern!"

"You used the Itzcoatal! That means they made it back. You see, three Aztecs helped me build it, and I taught them how to operate it. We made many voyages of exploration trying to find a way out of Aztlan. Then we realized that if we just followed certain currents, they would take us to the surface of a lake in another dome that appeared to be just above Aztlan. We made several trips there and even had an adventure with the king of a group of people living there."

Princess Portia jumped to her feet. "Those were my people!" she exclaimed. "I'm from the Aurora Dome, and the Itzcoatal brought the Sapphire Sword to King Duncan. That sword saved my people from being wiped out by the giant Basalt Beetles! Tell me how that all came about!"

"I want to know that, too," interrupted Percy, "but let's hear about it some other time. I think you'd better finish telling us what we need to know about your problems."

"Of course," agreed Portia with a sigh. "That can wait."

So, you're from that dome," mused Uncle. "Well, well, well, that is amazing. All these coincidences make me think that maybe the two of you can, indeed, help us. But to get back to my history, we made one other trip to Portia's dome after the adventure of the Sapphire Sword. On that trip I left my three Aztec companions and found my way back to the Earth's surface. I felt certain they would find their way back to Aztlan, but figured they would never use the Itzcoatal again, because the Aztec people didn't want to return to the surface. And, besides, they were a little afraid of the Itzcoatal. They thought it was magic. The most they wanted was to get the treasure and records. I wonder, did they ever do that, do you know?"

"They didn't," answered Percy. "The treasure still remains where you left it."

"Ah, so it was never retrieved or found," sighed Uncle. "Well, I suppose that's just as well. But, to get back to my story. When I got back to the surface, I found myself in a land that by the vegetation and climate appeared to be north of the Aztec treasure cave. I guessed that by Earth time several hundred years had passed since the Aztec war with the Spaniards. Yet there were no settlements or people within sight of where I was. I decided to begin walking southwest, knowing that I would eventually find somebody.

"I walked for months, always in a southwest direction, over mountains and through deserts, feeling that the surest way of finding civilization would be in that direction. And I was right, for eventually I came to the Pacific Ocean and the Spanish settlement of San Diego. If it hadn't been for my defective MiniGen, I would never have survived. It provided me with food and water, and even clothes. When my clothes got worn and ragged, I made new ones, conjuring up garments resembling those Aztecs wore. This was a mistake, for when the Catholic priests saw me, they took me for some wild savage unlike any they had ever seen before, and threw me in prison.

"Well, when they learned that I spoke Spanish, for I had downloaded the language from the mind of Cortez himself, they released me. I told them I was a Spaniard and had been captured many years before by Indians while traveling with missionaries from Mexico. That led to my being taken to Spain by the next ship going that way.

"From there I spent many years wandering about Europe and England, working as a traveling physician. Of course, I learned all the languages instantly and used my knowledge of medicine to cure many people."

"But," interrupted the Green Man, "you don't know anything about medicine!"

"My dear nephew, everybody knows a little bit about medicine, and I knew more, being from a more advanced planet, than the peoples of Europe. And I supplemented my knowledge from local books on medicine and herbs.

"I did that for many, many years and truly enjoyed myself. You may not know it, but this is a fascinating planet – the most fascinating I've ever been to in all my extensive travels. It's unique, and after you've been here awhile, it enchants you. Anyway, I eventually grew tired of being a traveling physician, and over a hundred years ago I came to America. I still enjoyed the traveling life, so I became a peddler. I got a horse and wagon and went from small town to small village along the east coast of the United States, selling all sorts of things, mainly pots and pans, clothing, bolts of cloth, and books, lots of books. For a while I sold nothing but books. What a wonderful life it was, meeting all those people.

"One day I visited a town where a circus had just set up their tents the day before, and I went to my first circus! That's all it took! I gave up my book peddling business right then and joined the circus! I did many things in the circus, roustabout, lion trainer, clown, and, finally, circus manager."

"My goodness, you've had an interesting life," observed Portia.

"Yeah," whistled Pouncer. "When I grow up, I want to be a lion in the circus. Maybe he can train me to be one."

Uncle, of course, couldn't understand Pouncer because he hadn't downloaded mountain lion into his mind, so he ignored Pouncer and told Portia that, indeed, he had had an interesting life, and he wasn't even relating a small part of all the adventures he had had.

"The circus," he continued, "is how I eventually met Barney. The last circus I managed was owned by Barney's grandfather. Barney was just a small boy when I met him. By the time the circus closed, Barney was a young man, and we were both looking for something to do. We both had been fascinated by the UFO phenomenon that had been sweeping the country for many years. I eventually told him who I really was and we came up with the idea of sponsoring and promoting UFO conferences, and eventually, UFO conventions. We co-own this company called UFO Attractions Unlimited."

"Well, I'm glad you told us this," said the Green Man. "Now I understand why you never returned to Kolobro and what you've been doing all this time. So, because you two are in charge of this convention, you don't want to come with me. Is that it?"

"That's part of it," said Uncle, "but it's much more than that. You see, I like it here, and I'm not sure I'm ready to leave yet. But I'm glad you're here because I've missed you and all the family. By being here you've provided me with a way back when I want to go, and you can tell the family all that I've told you."

Uncle paused as he tried to collect his thoughts so he could explain all the other complications. "You see," he continued, "Barney and I are broke. Our last few conventions didn't make any money. In fact, they lost money. Unless we can make a success of this one, we'll be out of business for good. In order to make this one a success we need to come up with a *hook*. A *hook* is something unusual, exciting, mysterious that will draw people in. We haven't come up with that yet, and the convention begins tomorrow.

"But there's more. To make matters worse, Janet Tono is here, and she might close us down before the convention is even over. She's from the government, the Department of Homeland Security, and she's positive we're harboring aliens from UFOs. She says if she finds any proof that we are, she'll not only close us down, but arrest us!"

"But you're not harboring any aliens, are you? I mean, aside from yourself," asked Percy.

For the first time Barney spoke. "That's just the trouble. We are, in a kind of a sort of a way. You see, what we've discovered over the years, and we wouldn't have if it hadn't been for Adam, is that UFO aliens are attracted to UFO conventions. They come to them to see what other aliens are on Earth, and to see what humans really know about them."

"You mean there are lots of aliens on Earth besides Uncle and the Green Man?" exclaimed Percy.

"I'm afraid so," said Barney rather sadly.

"But you said," complained the Green Man, "that Earth was an insignificant planet, and no one wanted to visit it. That's why you chose to come here."

"On Kolobro," explained Uncle, "it's an insignificant, uninteresting planet, but on other planets in the galaxy it's a curiosity."

"Well, how many other aliens are there here?" asked Portia, dumbfounded to discover that the Outworld had so many people from other planets. When the Green Man appeared, she was amazed to find that another planet contained people, but now she was almost overwhelmed to discover there were many inhabited planets.

"We don't know," said Barney, "but so far there are only two that have registered for this convention."

"Two that we know of," added Uncle. "We don't always know that aliens are aliens. Sometimes I know by the way they behave, but sometimes I don't. It's hard to tell."

"Yeah," said Barney. "Everybody acts weird at these conventions."

"The Beamus twins, they're the two aliens we know of at this convention," explained Uncle, "and they're real oddballs. From what I've been able to figure out, they're stranded on this planet, too. They're looking to hitch a ride with someone back to their home planet. That makes them really nosey. They question everyone they meet to see if they are aliens, too. Of course, they don't want Janet Tono to know they're aliens, but they can't seem to help making spectacles of themselves, so they're bound to give themselves away eventually. If they do, then they'll throw suspicion on everybody."

"Do they know Uncle is an alien?" asked Percy.

" Not yet, but they're likely to find out sometime and put him in danger. They are always loud and noisy, and always seem to draw attention to themselves," added Barney.

"We're afraid that Janet Tono and her henchman are finally going to take notice of them and bring them in for questioning. Then they might give themselves away and get us arrested for harboring them even if they don't know who I really am!" explained Uncle.

"Well,s then, it's good they don't know you're an alien," said Percy.

"They come to all the conventions, and I think they suspect me, but they don't know for sure. And if Janet Tono doesn't find out who they are, Lou Lonewolf may. He's already suspicious. And if he finds out, Tono will know, too!"

Portia was about to ask who Lou Lonewolf was when Uncle blurted out, "But there's another problem, the biggest problem of all. My MiniGen is missing! If Janet Tono gets hold of that, we're finished, and who knows what will happen to me! Percy and Portia, the thing you could really do to help us is find that MiniGen!"

"Hey, I'm good at finding things," whistled Pouncer. "My smeller is a thousand times better than a human's!"

"So let me get all these problems and things straight," began Percy. "Number one, you like it here and really don't want to leave with the Green Man. Number two, the convention isn't making any money, so you're going broke and need to find a way to make some dough. Number three, this Janet Tono is out to get you and the convention. Number four, the Beamus twins and this Lonewolf guy may also cause trouble. And, Number five, you've lost your MiniGen!"

"That about covers it," sighed Uncle. "Like I said, Percy, maybe you could find the MiniGen, but I don't really see how you can help with the other things."

"Now, don't underestimate Percy, he's a most remarkable boy!" stated the Green Man. "It so happens that I wouldn't be here today if it wasn't for him. I most likely would have been trapped in a horrible place inside the earth!"

"Yes, Uncle," agreed Portia. "There's no telling what Percy can do."

Chapter 6

Percy and Portia attend the UFO convention

Here we go again, thought Percy. Portia and the Green Man expect me to perform miracles. Just because I got lucky a few times, and got us out of some fixes, doesn't mean I can solve everybody's problems. Uncle's problems are grown-up problems and stuff that I have no idea how to solve. I don't even know how to begin to find the MiniGen. I really wish I'd never come here!

But he was here, in Phoenix, Arizona, at a UFO convention, so he knew he'd have to try to do something. He looked helplessly at Uncle and Barney and then said to the Green Man, "Didn't you say that you located Uncle by tracking the signal coming from his MiniGen? Couldn't you do just the same and find wherever it is around here?"

The Green Man's face beamed, and he slapped his forehead, sending his black waves of hair rippling. "Well, of course. Why didn't I think of that. All I have to do is make some adjustments, and we'll have it tracked down in no time!"

He fished a MiniGen out of his shoulder bag and began adjusting the dome on one end. (For those of you who have failed to read *Percy Fitz and the Green Man Mystery*, and wonder what a MiniGen is, it's a clear crystal tube about eight inches long and an inch in diameter. Inside it is a black sphere, about the size of a pea. On the outside is a button that can be slid in any direction, and this button moves the black sphere around. Each end is capped with a clear crystal dome with spiderweb-like lines all over it. How does it work? Who knows!) He then slid the button to a certain position and pointed the other end of the MiniGen in the air. He slowly walked around in a circle. Nothing happened.

"I don't understand," complained the Green Man. "I should be getting a beeping sound. Maybe I made the wrong adjustments."

"No," said Uncle. "It's not your adjustments. I forgot to tell you that there's another defect in my MiniGen. It sometimes doesn't work at all. It's as if it has batteries, and the batteries have run down. Then after a while they recharge themselves again and the thing works for a while longer. The last time it worked was just before you arrived, nephew. It must have run down soon after that."

"Well, how long does it take to recharge?" Percy asked.

"There's no telling. Sometimes it's two or three days; sometimes longer. Maybe a week or more," explained Uncle.

Percy ran this fingers through his red hair, the

same way that King Priam always did when he was puzzled or frustrated, and then asked Uncle how he had lost the MiniGen and where he had seen it last. Uncle said he had last seen it in the bathroom. He smiled a broad winning smile, much like the one the Green Man had, and said, "You see, I love bubble baths. Bubble baths are one of my weaknesses, and the MiniGen can make the best bubble soap found on any planet. I left it sitting on the edge of the tub. That was yesterday. I didn't notice it was gone until this afternoon."

"I don't like baths," whistled Pouncer.

"You've never had a bath," stated Portia, "so how would you know you don't like them."

"I just know," whistled Pouncer and shook his head.

"So," said Percy, "someone had to steal it from the edge of the tub. Who's been in this room besides you and Barney?"

"We had two meetings with presenters yesterday," said Uncle, "one in the morning and one in the afternoon. I know that the MiniGen was there after the morning meeting because I saw it."

"Then in the afternoon there was the maid," said Barney, "and then after her we had a conference with many other presenters to go over some details of the convention before it officially gets started tomorrow morning. Lou Lonewolf, Becky Moon, Jake Noory, Steve Woods,   and James Cameron were here for that."

"So any one of those people could have taken it," suggested Percy. "One of them must have. Who are they, and do you suspect any one of them?"

"We don't suspect any of them," said Uncle. "They wouldn't know what it was, and I don't see why any of them would take it. Ufologists don't steal things!"

"Percy's right to suspect them," said Barney. "It has to be one of them. I don't think the maid would dare take anything. She'd get in too much trouble and lose her job. I don't see how it could be one of the others, but let me tell you about them."

Barney dabbed the perspiration on his mustache with a paper napkin and proceeded to describe the five. "Lou Lonewolf is a professional blogger. He writes up the convention for his blog, *UFO X-Files.* He comes to all the conventions and gets stories. He's a weird guy, but to steal the MiniGen, I don't think so."

"That's a good reason to steal it," interjected Percy. "What a great story that would be! 'Blogger finds object from another world!' He'd become world famous!"

Barney and Uncle both agreed. "Then," continued Barney, "there's Becky Moon. This is her first convention. It was a great bit of luck to get her to come speak. She just wrote a book called *By Invitation.* It's all about her encounter with a UFO, how she was invited inside of it, and what happened in there. But I can't see her taking it. She wouldn't have any idea what it was."

"Maybe she saw something similar inside the UFO," suggested Percy. "She might know it was something from outer space. Having it might help her sell books."

"That's true!" exclaimed Barney. "Man, what a sales gimmick that would be! She could say that it was proof positive that she had actually been on a UFO!"

"Kolobro is the only planet with MiniGens. She couldn't have seen one inside a UFO," stated the Green Man.

"You're right," agreed Uncle. "As far as we know, no other planet has Generatus, but I have seen crystal cylinders on other planets that are used as batteries."

"Well, it sounds as if she might have a motive then," said Portia. "But, as Percy said, this Lou Lonewolf would have a strong motive, too."

"What about the others?" asked Percy.

"James Cameron is a professor of astrophysics and an expert on ufology. He'll be speaking on that subject. Jake Noory is an historian. He'll be speaking on the Roswell UFO crash and what new information has come to light. And Steve Woods, he's a former scientist who worked at Area 51. He'll be speaking on what he saw at that super-secret government installation," said Barney. "For him, like the other two, stealing the MiniGen would be absolute proof that UFO's really do exist."

"So that means everybody but the maid had a motive to steal it!" sighed Portia.

"I don't," whistled Pouncer. "It would taste like glass, and glass tastes nasty." Everyone ignored him, so he leaped on an overstuffed chair and went to sleep.

Percy ran the fingers of both hands through his hair again. He felt frustrated and overwhelmed. There were just too many problems, and he was just a kid. Really, what could he do for all these adults? Why couldn't he just solve "kid" kind of problems?

"Look, I'm just a kid," he complained. "I'd like to help, but I think this is all too much for me."

"But, Percy, you figured out a way to get us out of those horrible Rings," observed the Green Man, "and that was worse than this stuff. Surely you can think of something that would help!"

"You're right, Percy, that's a lot to ask. But the Green Man's right, too. You did get us out of The Rings, and that was brilliant. Let's just start with the MiniGen, like Uncle suggested," soothed Portia. "How could we find out who has the MiniGen? Let's just start with that. That's the biggest problem, but it may be the easiest to solve. Let's just start with finding out who has it. You know, since we're here, we should try something."

Portia's melodious, reassuring voice had a calming effect on Percy. Yes, he thought, his blood pressure returning to normal, since we're here it won't

66

hurt to try something, but what?

"Well, first of all, I think any of them would suspect that it wasn't from this world so that was a reason for taking it. Next, I think whoever has it will wait until a time when it's most advantageous for them to reveal it. Probably during their presentation at the convention."

"Lou Lonewolf wouldn't want to reveal it during the convention. He'd want to wait until it was over and then reveal it on his blog. He'd want to tell some story about how he got it during the convention," said Uncle.

"Yeah," added Barney. "And none of the presenters would want Janet Tono and that bozo muscleman of hers, Tom Gerry, to get hold of it before their revelation. And they're going to have a plan to disappear from the convention right after their presentation so they don't get arrested for possessing and hiding an alien artifact."

"Now that I'm thinking about it," mused Uncle, " If I were a presenter, I wouldn't reveal it during my presentation. It would be too easy for Janet Tono to arrest me. I'd make some reference to it, some hint about it, and then reveal it later when it would be easier to escape Tono's clutches."

"So that means we need to search their rooms as soon as possible," said Percy.

"But what if they haven't hidden it in their rooms?" asked Portia. "MiniGens are small enough to be carried with you, and nobody would notice."

Uncle, the Green Man, Barney, and Percy, all of whom had begun to get excited about a plan coming together, sank back in their chairs and were silent. It was obvious they couldn't bodily search all the suspects.

Pouncer, who had been curled up in a chair, comfortably dozing and listening, suddenly whistled, very casually, "I can smell it."

"What did he say?" asked Uncle.

"I think he's saying he can smell the MiniGen," said the Green Man.

"Yeah, I can smell it. You remember, Percy and Portia, back in Aurora when we were all trying to figure out what was causing all those weird things. My dad and mom first noticed a strange smell. Then I did, too. It was kind of like the smell that comes off old metal cans that have been left in the sun. Well, we later realized it was coming from the Transporter Gen. Since then I've noticed that the MiniGens give off that same smell."

"What'd he say?" asked Barney, also not understanding mountain lion.

Percy explained and then asked Pouncer if MiniGens smell even if they weren't working. "Sure, they smell all the time. It's like the crystal they're made of has soaked up the smell," Pouncer explained, as if he were a big authority on smells.

"Well then, the first thing we have to do is get

Pouncer to smell all the suspects," said Portia. "See, Percy, you've got us started on a plan already!"

"It was my idea," whistled Pouncer.

"Of course, it was," agreed Portia, "you and Percy together."

"So now what we need to do," said Uncle, "is get Pouncer to smell all the suspects."

"That will be easy. I'll just call them all up here right now. Tell them we just want to be double sure everything is okay," said Barney. "Maybe having them altogether will not only allow Pouncer to smell them, but one of 'em might get real nervous. That might help us be extra sure who it is."

"You know," mused Percy, "it's too bad there isn't an alien artifact that could be shown during the convention. Not a real alien artifact. We wouldn't want Janet Tono arresting anyone, but something strange that could be mistaken for one. Something that would make people want to come to the convention. Something that would be sure to bring a big crowd in and make you guys tons of money!"

"Say!" exclaimed Barney, "that gives me an idea! What if we kept Lou here after the others left and said we had a question for him. We'd say we had heard rumors going around that there was a big surprise going to be announced sometime during the convention. We'd say we didn't know what it was, but it was some sort of absolute proof of UFOs. You see what I mean, Adam. Give him some story that's all vague and everything.   Then ask him if he knew anything about it!"

"Yes, I see what you're driving at." said Uncle. "He'd really go for something like that. He'd have it out on his blog within an hour. Everybody who cares about ufology reads his blog ten times a day. People in the Phoenix area would pile in here to see what was going to be announced!"

"And we wouldn't be lying to him, because we said it was just a rumor," added Barney.

"Furthermore," said Uncle, grimly, "unless we can stop it, an alien artifact will be revealed."

Portia beamed. "That was brilliant, Percy, you gave Barney a great idea!"

Chapter 7

What alien beings really look like

While Barney began calling the suspects, Uncle sat down at the computer and printed off convention badges for Percy, Portia, and the Green Man. When he came to America he had given himself the name Adam Green. He decided upon this name because he was the first man from Kolobro to come to this planet, and he had worn a green suit just like the Green Man's. Now, as he typed up and printed off the badges, he took the liberty of giving his nephew and friends new names as well. The Green Man became Junior Green, Percy became Percy Green, and Portia became Portia Green. Since Portia had said that the name of her city was Aurora, Uncle made their place of residence Aurora, Colorado, because he knew there was an Aurora, Colorado.

As an example, Portia's badge read:

Portia Green
Aurora, Colorado
Desert Wind Hotel and Convention Center
10th Annual UFO Convention – Southwest
Region

Uncle attached lanyards and hung them around

their necks. He then stood back and eyed all four critically. "Pizflicofimacax, your name is now Junior Green, and if anyone asks, these two are your cousins, and I'm still your uncle. Portia and Percy, you're now brother and sister. You've all come to the convention to see what it's like and to visit me, your uncle. You're dressed as you are because you love Becky Moon's book, *By Invitation*, and you wanted to look like the characters in her book. You actually look remarkably like the characters in her book except for those corkscrew spirals, but that won't matter. Now, as for Pouncer, we'll have to do something about him. In her book there's a creature called a Flixlun. It looks pretty much like Pouncer except it has black ears and a black tail."

Uncle went to his bedroom and returned with a makeup case. In it was a small spray bottle of black paint. In a moment Pouncer's ears and tail were black. Uncle held out a mirror for him to see himself. He was pleased. He thought he looked better than ever before. He strutted around the room, leaped over the couch, and came back to look at himself in the mirror again.

Barney made the calls, and within fifteen minutes all the suspects were gathered in the suite. First came Lou Lonewolf. He was about thirty years old, tall and thin, with straight, unwashed brown hair that hung nearly to his shoulders. His face, like his frame, was thin, and he had a haggard, worried look, a look that had become permanent with him because of all the government conspiracies and rumors of alien abductions and UFO takeovers he dealt with on a daily basis.

"Thanks for inviting me to these meetings," he said, as he shook Uncle's hand. "It always gives me good stuff for my blog. Even people who can't come to the conventions love to hear all about what happens at them."

Jake Norry , the Roswell expert, arrived next. (Roswell, New Mexico, is a place where a UFO crashed a long time ago, and the Army found some dead aliens.) He was a small, thin man, with a pale, unhealthy complexion and large glasses with dark frames. "I hope this won't take long," he grumbled. "I have people I need to meet in ten minutes."

Steve Woods, the speaker on Area 51, came in right behind Jake. (Area 51 is a super-secret military base in Nevada. No one is allowed to go anywhere near there except some scientists.) He was a well-groomed young man in an expensive suit. He looked more like a successful businessman than someone deeply interested in alien encounters. He sat down on the couch next to Jake and seemed very pleased and happy.

Next arrived James Cameron, who was going to speak on ufology. He was an older man with trifocal glasses and an untrimmed beard. He did seem nervous about something, and once he had come in and closed the door, he paused in the middle of the room, went back to the door, opened it, and looked out again.

Becky Moon, the author of the best-selling *By Invitation*, was the last to arrive. She was a young woman in her twenties. She looked a little bewildered and unhappy. Her most remarkable feature was her silver hair. She had straight, medium-length hair that her stylist, if she had one, would call platinum blonde. To anyone else, however, it was silver.

Uncle thanked them all for coming and introduced the Green Man, Percy, Portia and Pouncer, and explained they were his relatives. He then explained that he wanted to be doubly sure he had gotten everything right, just in case he had to send out a revised program. While this was going on, Pouncer went playfully up to each one of them and carefully sniffed.

When this was all done and everyone agreed the agenda was correct, they all quickly filed out but Lou and Becky. Lou lingered because Barney asked him to, and Becky seemed very curious about Uncle's family.

"Thank you for dressing up for the convention," she said to Portia and Percy. "Your costumes look very authentic except for the gold corkscrews. Why did you put those on your robes? Of course, there were several of my aliens with gold infinity signs on their robes, but I didn't put that in my book. It's very strange that you should have gold symbols on your robes."

Barney came over and said, taking her by the arm, "Well thank you for coming, Becky; we'll see you later. He then pushed her out the door and closed it. "The less said on that topic, the better," he added.

"What is it you wanted to talk to me about?" asked Lou, fingering his iPad.

"Thanks for sticking around," began Uncle, trying to put Lou at ease. "It's just that we were wondering if you've heard any rumors going around the convention? There's always rumors of course, and I know that it hasn't actually started yet, but we were wondering if you'd heard anything, you know, kind of unusual."

"He means more unusual than normal," added Barney.

Lou raised his thin eyebrows and looked at them suspiciously. "No, nothing unusual. Just the same old stuff. There's rumors of alien beings attending the convention, but there's that at all the conventions. Nothing ever seems to come of it."

"Nothing else?" asked Barney.

"No."

"It's just that we've heard rumors. Well, maybe not rumors. Maybe just hints that there's going to be a surprise revealed sometime during this convention," Uncle confided.

"Now, we personally don't have any surprises, and no one's told us they have a surprise, but you know how things, or hints of things, have a way of getting around these conventions," added Barney in a vague sort of way.

"Well, what are you talking about?" asked Lou, getting excited. "I need to know. I'm the press. I need to tell everyone if there's something unusual going to happen."

"Like I said, it's just a sort of rumor," continued Uncle, "but the word going round is there's going to be some sort of proof of UFOs revealed sometime during the next two days."

"You mean something like an alien artifact? Who's going to do it?" exclaimed Lou. "Are you sure about this? I mean, if this is true, it could be the biggest story I've ever had!"

"Well, we don't know if it's true," cautioned Barney, "but if it is, I'm sure there would be plenty of people who'd want to be the first to report it to the world."

"I'm going to put something on my blog about this. I'll just list it as a rumor, but if it is true, then I'll be the first one to break the story. Boy! Is this big!" Clutching his iPad, he rushed from the room.

Uncle and Barney smiled and shook hands. Now that they were alone, they all looked enquiringly at Pouncer.

"Well, Pouncer, what did you smell?" asked Portia.

"They all smelled weird," whistled Pouncer. "That Becky had a sweet smell, and Lou smelled like smoke."

"She means," said Percy, "did you smell the MiniGen on any of them?"

"Nope, none of them have the MiniGen on them."

"Well, the way Lou reacted when we mentioned the alien artifact, I'd say it's obvious he doesn't have it," observed Uncle.

The Green Man, who had been silent and watching the proceedings for a long time now, looked over at Percy. His green suit peeked out of the front of his shirt collar, and he looped his finger in it and tugged, as if to loosen it from around his neck. "Well what next, Percy? Should we start searching rooms?"

"Let's just wait a minute," Uncle said before Percy could answer. He had a computer tablet in his hand and was intently watching the screen. "I'm on Lou's blog, ALIEN X-FILES. I want to see if he posts something about what we said."

Sure enough, after about ten minutes something appeared. "EXCITING NEWS! As you all know, your reporter, Lonewolf, is here at the 10th annual UFO convention in Phoenix. I always hesitate to report rumors, but in this case I felt compelled to because, if this one turns out to be true, it could be the biggest story in history! A low whispering has begun circulating among the participants of this convention, which officially begins tomorrow, that someone, perhaps one of the presenters, is going to reveal a genuine **alien artifact**! I have a secret inside source who has verified this rumor. My source can't say who the presenter is, and is being very mysterious and circumspect about the whole thing. Any of my readers who are in the Phoenix area should attend this conference if at all possible. It could be a once-in-a-lifetime opportunity. For those of you who can't attend, keep logged on! Depend on me to reveal all just as it happens!"

"I think Lou Lonewolf exaggerated a bit on what you guys told him," said Percy dryly.

"By all the Jovian moons, that's what I was hoping he would do! That story should bring in droves of convention goers!" exclaimed Barney. "We'll not only pay for this convention, but even pay off some of our other bills! Your Percy here is a genius!"

"Maybe," cautioned Uncle, "but if we don't get that MiniGen back, and whoever has it does reveal it, then we're doomed. We're out of business and may even go to jail. Janet Tono will force whoever has it to tell where they got it. We'll both be arrested for harboring an alien object, and maybe even be charged for having an alien weapon! Tono may even find out who I really am!"

"We will just have to search the rooms right now and find it!" stated Portia.

"No, it's too late in the day to search the rooms now. Everybody will be in their rooms by this time of night," explained Uncle. "We'll have to wait until tomorrow when everybody's in meetings."

They all agreed to wait and decided it was time they, too, turned in. Uncle had Barney move into his room, and directed Percy and Junior to take one bed in Barney's room, and Portia and Pouncer to take the other. Portia had never slept in a king- or even a queen-sized bed before, and Pouncer had never slept in any real bed before.

The Green Man slipped into bed, lay on his back, closed his eyes, and was immediately asleep. Percy lay on his side, staring at the red glow of the clock and the yellow light that filtered through the window curtain. He wasn't at all sleepy and kept wondering why he had agreed to come here. It would have been all right if he had come here just to enjoy the convention and explain it to the Green Man. That would have been fun. He thought about the morning and how they could go about searching the rooms. What if they got arrested, which was a good possibility. The situation would be even worse if that happened. He wasn't so worried about himself as he was for Portia, the Green Man and Uncle. The police would probably find out that Portia was from Aurora. Then what would happen to Aurora? What would happen to the others if it was discovered that they were from another planet? Would they be dissected like frogs?

He rolled to his other side and began resenting the Green Man and Uncle, and why they just didn't solve their own problems. After all, they probably had over a thousand years of experience between them. He sighed deeply and realized he was tired and making more of the issues than he needed to. He would just try to relax and take things as they came; after all, he could only do what he could do. He closed his eyes and was asleep before he knew it.

Meanwhile, Pouncer leaped on his bed but didn't get under the covers. He screwed his head under the big pillow, then tossed it into the air, and it landed at the foot of the bed. Springing to his feet, he leaped on it, rolled over, tossed it into the air again – it landed at the foot of the bed again -- and then got into a desperate wrestling match with it. He growled quietly and slammed into Portia. She grabbed him by the ear and warned him to be quiet and settle down. He said okay and then nosed his way under the covers. Then he crawled to the bottom of the bed and back up again, finally coming to rest with all four paws against Portia's back. Soon he was making a noise between a snore and a purr.

Portia, however, was like Percy. She couldn't go directly to sleep. She was thinking about what a strange and confusing world the Outworld was, and how she wasn't at all sure she liked it. She thought perhaps it was because she wasn't used to it. But from the little she had seen, she liked the places where there were few people and lots of nature, like Pan Woods. She was sorry for Percy. He seemed overwhelmed by all he was asked to do. It was a lot. She smiled in her pillow, thinking how brilliant he was, and how he never realized it. He always thought that all the good outcomes he was involved with were mostly good luck, but she knew the good outcomes would never have happened if Percy hadn't been there. Look how this rumor about the alien artifact had worked out. That wouldn't have happened without Percy's off the wall comment. She gently slid over to get away from Pouncer's paws. He slid forward so he could feel her back again.

Chapter 8

What ufology is anyway?

At 8:00 a.m. the next morning everyone was awake and gathered round the conference table in Uncle's room. Juice for everyone and a bowl of milk for Pouncer were delivered by room service. On the agenda was a plan for searching all the suspects' rooms. The suspects had been narrowed to four: Becky Moon, Jake Noory, Steven Woods, and James Cameron. Percy felt a little better about things, it being morning and a bright desert sun shining through the window. But he was still worried about everyone getting arrested, and expressed his concern and the possible consequences to everybody.

"Yes," agreed Uncle, "that is a worry. Janet Tono already suspects everyone, and she, too, will have read Lou's blog. That will make her even more suspicious and watchful."

"And how can we know for sure that no one's in the room we're searching?" asked Portia. "It all sounds so very risky."

Percy looked down at the agenda Uncle had passed around . The first item read, "9:00 - 10:00 AM Breakfast in Gila Room (tickets required), Speaker,

James Cameron discusses Ufology, an Overview."

"Well," observed Percy, "one thing's for sure; James Cameron won't be in his room between nine and ten."

"Say, that's it!" exclaimed Barney. "We'll start with James and search his room between nine and ten! But we all won't do it, just me. I'm no alien, and if I get caught, it won't be as bad."

"You should take Pouncer with you," said Percy. "If the MiniGen is there, he'll be able to sniff it out."

"I'll sniff it out in a flash," whistled Pouncer. "They can't hide it anywhere that I won't find it."

"What about me? I want to do something," said the Green Man.

"You can be the lookout," said Barney.

"Yes, I'll be the lookout." The Green Man smiled his wide, beautifully-teethed smile. "Just exactly what is a lookout?" he added.

"You just wander up and down the hall outside James' room while we're in it. If you see anyone coming down the hall, start whistling, and Pouncer and I'll hide," explained Barney.

"Got it," grinned the Green Man, happy to be part of the action. "Just whistle any old tune, I suppose?" Barney nodded.

"Portia, Percy and I will go to the meeting," said Uncle. "That way we can keep an eye on Cameron. It's also customary for either Barney or me to be at all presentations. If one of us isn't there, it might arouse somebody's suspicions."

He handed Percy and Portia a breakfast ticket, and they went down to the Gila Room. The Gila Room was on the main floor, just to the right of the convention registration desk. The entire lobby area was crowded with people. There was hardly room to move through the milling mass. Lines at the registration desk went out the hotel's front door. The Gila Room itself was already full, and waiters were putting up extra tables. There was one reserved near the front for VIP's and Uncle led Portia and Percy to it. Lou Lonewolf, Becky Moon, and James Cameron were already seated at it.

Percy felt uneasy as they made their way to the table. It seemed to him that many people were staring at them. He wondered if those posters with his photo on them were still circulating around and had found their way as far south as Phoenix. Then he realized they weren't staring at him, but were staring at Portia. It suddenly occurred to him that she really did stand out in a crowd. She had a very regal bearing, walking erect with her head up, her long strawberry-blonde hair swaying, and her large green eyes unblinking. Her appearance was striking even in such an odd assortment of people. Portia herself didn't seem to notice.

Waitresses and waiters were weaving their way among the tables, delivering plates of steaming omelets and hash brown potatoes. Portia's eyes widened (which didn't seem possible her eyes being so remarkably large anyway) as a plate was lowered in front of her. She took a bite of the ham and cheese omelet and smiled dreamily.

"This is lovely," she said. (In the Netherworld there are no eggs, and thus no omelets.) "The one good thing about the Outworld is the food. It's all lovely!"

When Uncle finished eating, he walked to the nearby raised podium, tapped on the microphone, and began to speak.

"I'm Adam Green, your host for the 10th annual UFO convention for the Southwest region. As most of you know, UFO conventions differ from UFO conferences in that they are less serious and scholarly and much more fun! (Applause) You can see this by all the attendees in costumes we have here! (More applause)

"As you can see from your programs, we have some interesting speakers and exhibits during the next two days, and, who knows, there might even be some surprises. (Murmurs throughout the audience) Now, I'd like to introduce to you our first speaker, James Cameron.

James teaches sociology at Arizona State University and has been fascinated by UFOs since his boyhood. This morning he will give us an overview of the science of ufology."

As the audience applauded between bites of omelet, James Cameron came to the podium. "Good morning. I'm happy to be here with you this morning to discuss my favorite topic. Let's start with what ufology is. As I'm sure we all know, ufology is the study of unidentified flying objects and all things related to them. This morning I wish to begin by describing the beings on these UFOs, and speculate on why they are here.

"By compiling the descriptions given to us by people who have been abducted, or, who otherwise encountered extraterrestrials, we have so far been able to identify five types or species of beings, but it is likely there are more. First, what seems to be the most common type are the Amphibians. Their skin is like a frog's, smooth and clammy. It varies in color, some saying it is green others white, and still others brown. They are between four- and five-feet tall, have short arms, and three fingers on each hand.

"The next most common type is the Greys. The Greys are biological robots or androids. They are tall and thin, with large black eyes. They have two nostril slits where a nose should be, with long, egg-shaped heads. They are hairless. Of all the types, the Greys seemed to be the most intimidating and aggressive.

"Next we have the Non-greys. The Non-greys appear similar to the Greys, but are child-like in size and appearance. They have fair, pale skin, bald heads, large, bulging eyes, thin lips, and a high forehead.

"The least common are the Giants. Giants are eight feet tall or taller. They are of slender build with fine, thin hair covering the entire body and face. They seemed to be the most curious of the five classifications. They are shy and non-aggressive.

"The last type, and the type I find the most intriguing is the Nordics. They intrigue me the most because they are most like us. So much like us, in fact, that they can walk among us unnoticed. Who knows but some may be in this audience. Who knows but one may be sitting next to you right now! Nordics look human but tend to be very fair of complexion and have blonde hair and bright green or blue eyes. It is my opinion that the alien beings Becky Moon encountered and described in her book, *By Invitation,* were of the Nordic variety.

"We will discuss these five types in more detail later on, but let's take a moment to conjecture why these alien beings in their spaceships are visiting our planet. Why have they come to Earth? There are five major explanations. The first is a benign, harmless reason. They are lost in space. They are explorers who have lost their way and are trying to get back to their home planet. This seems unlikely to me. Second, they are vacationers, here on holiday in the same way you or I would go to Hawaii! That might be a distant possibility. Third, they are time travelers, coming here from our past or our future, or both. Perhaps some of them are ourselves from a future time. Perhaps some of them are humans who have evolved into a different species! A fascinating possibility.

Fourth, they are here to colonize Earth. Perhaps their planet is dying or over populated. Whatever the reason, it's not a pleasant thought. Colonization could well mean the end of the human race, or, if not the end, the enslavement of all humans! But the fifth reason is the most chilling and sinister of all, *Intervention*. They are here to interfere with, to mettle with the human race. Perhaps they even originally designed humans, and they are here watching us, seeing what and how we are doing. Perhaps they are planning to make adjustments in us by, say, altering our DNA, or in other ways changing our evolutionary future."

Let us leave Mr. Cameron and his fascinating talk on ufology and travel to the 7th floor of the hotel, where we find Barney, Pouncer, and the Green Man standing in front of room number 704. Now nobody had considered how they were going to get into room 704 without a key until they were standing there before it. The Green Man, not knowing the customs and procedures of getting into hotel rooms, pulled, pushed, and twisted the door handle, and nothing happened. He rattled it several times. Still nothing happened.

"We need the key," Barney whispered by way of explanation.

"Where is it?" the Green Man whispered back.

"We don't have it. We won't be able to get in."

The Green Man smiled his winning smile and

pulled from his shoulder bag a MiniGen. (He wasn't ever without his shoulder bag, even with his Earthman clothes on.) He made several quick adjustments on it, pointed it at the lock, and pushed the button. There was a slight click, and the green light came on. Barney pulled down the handle, and they all three quickly entered the room.

"No," said Barney, pushing the Green Man toward the door. "You're supposed to wait outside, you know, walk up and down the hall, and be our lookout, remember?"

"Oh, yes," said the Green Man, "of course, and I whistle if somebody's coming." He tipped-toed to the door and left.

When he was gone, Barney turned on the light and said to Pouncer, "Okay little feller, do your stuff. Find the MiniGen, and Uncle Barney will give you six cans of tuna for lunch. Pouncer whistled back that he wanted chicken for lunch, but Barney didn't understand mountain lion.

"Let's start with the bed," suggested Barney. "People often hide things in their bed. Come on, boy, let's sniff around here."

"I'm not a dog," whistled Pouncer, and then proceeded to pounce on the bed.

"No, no," said Barney, " don't jump on it. Now look, you've messed up the spread. This place has to look like no one's been here," he added, as he straightened the spread. Pouncer smelled around and under the bed and then went to the dresser and closet. His next stop was the bathroom. At that point they heard whistling outside. They both froze and waited. The whistling continued, but no one tried to open the door. Finally, Barney went over and gently opened it a crack. The Green Man was coming down the hall toward him, but nobody else was in sight.

"Why are you whistling?" hissed Barney. "There's nobody around!"

"Was I whistling?" asked the Green Man with a surprised look.

"Yes, you were whistling," growled Barney. "You're not supposed to whistle unless someone is coming!"

"Oh, right. I'll just whistle if someone is coming."

Barney pulled his head back in the room and closed the door, grumbling to himself. He returned to the bathroom and said, "Why are you drinking from the toilet, Pouncer? Don't you know better than that? It's unsanitary! You're supposed to be sniffing; get to sniffing!"

"I was thirsty," whistled Pouncer, "and sniffing makes me thirsty. Boy, are you a grouch! Sniff, sniff, sniff, that's all you think about."

Of course, Barney didn't understand Pouncer's reply, all he heard was soft whistling sounds. Pouncer sniffed around the bathroom some more, licking his whiskers and thinking how the water tasted cool and clean to him.

Finally, he whistled, "There's nothing here, no MiniGen," and walked to the door. Barney followed, not knowing what he whistled, but assuming they were both done.

Back in the Gila Room, Cameron was wrapping up his talk on ufology by describing the various shapes and physical attributes of UFO spacecraft. Percy and Portia had begun looking around them while they listened and had noticed a table off to their right that had something unusual about it. All the other tables were crowded with people, but this particular one had only two individuals seated at it. One was a woman. She was short and stout, with short, dark hair streaked with grey. Her eyes were dark, small and penetrating, and if her face expressed anything, it was suspicion. She glared at everyone from under heavy black eyebrows. Seated next to her was a large, muscle-bound, young man with light brown hair and kindly brown eyes to match. Whereas the woman was wearing a black business suit, he wore a very bright and flowery Hawaiian shirt.

Percy, noting that Portia was looking at the same odd couple, tapped Uncle on the arm and asked who they were.

"Ah," replied Uncle, "that's Janet Tono and her fellow agent, Tom Gerry. They're the ones we told you about from the Department of Homeland Security. Tono's the boss, and Gerry's what we call

91

her enforcer or bodyguard. Everybody knows who they are, and nobody will sit with them. They come to every convention thinking they're going to catch an alien or arrest somebody with secret information. So far they've found nothing, but they're making us all very nervous. And, as I said, if they get their hands on that MiniGen, it's all up for us!"

"She's really been staring at me," whispered Portia.

"Everyone's been staring at you," said Percy.

"Maybe, but not like her. It's not like she's curious; it's like she thinks I've done something."

At that moment Cameron completed his talk, and applause rattled through the room. People began looking at their programs as they filed out, deciding on which of the workshops and presentations they were going to attend before the dinner speech by Becky Moon. But before Uncle, Percy, and Portia could move away from the table, Janet Tono and Tom Gerry had parted the crowd and stood before them.

"It looks to be a good convention," said Tono in a husky voice. "We're looking forward to attending all of it."

"Thank you," was Uncle's brief reply.

"And who is this lovely young lady?" asked Tono, her face almost cracking in her attempt to smile.

"This is my niece and nephew, Portia Green and her brother, Percy. They've come all the way from Aurora to visit their old Uncle Adam and see what he does for a living. Who knows, they may even end up being my helpers."

"So, is this your first convention?" Tono asked.

"Yes," said Portia, taking Uncle's hand.

"Well, I didn't think I've seen you before. You may be in for an exciting convention. There are rumors going around that something unexpected is going to happen. It's said that something or someone alien is going to appear." Her head suddenly peered up at Uncle. "You wouldn't know anything about that, would you, Mr. Green?"

"Of course, I've heard the rumors," replied Uncle, trying his best to look innocent, "but I think they're just that, rumors. You know how these things are, some little thing is mentioned, and pretty soon it's blown all out of proportion. Somebody finds a rock or a crystal or something, and they think it's from another planet, when it's just an ordinary rock or crystal."

"So you've heard something about a rock or crystal?" demanded Tono.

"Why, no," exclaimed Uncle, stumbling back a step. "I, I was just using that as an example."

"I've made it perfectly clear in the past, and I'm sure you understand," glowered Tono, "that the Department of Homeland Security is responsible for the safety of this country from any possible enemies, whether they are from this planet or any other. If you know of anything we should know, you have a duty to inform us. I expect to hear from you about anything unusual that happens or will happen during this convention!" At this point she stared hard at Portia for about a minute but never seemed to notice Percy. Then she walked away, followed by Tom Gerry, who had not even tried to crack a smile or offer a comment or greeting during the entire encounter.

"She is about as scary as the Satyrs in Aurora!" shivered Portia.

"Yeah, and if she had horns, she'd pretty much look like one!" added Percy. "I've got a feeling we'd better stay way far away from those two!"

"She worries me, too," said Uncle. "I've never seen her so aggressive. That blog message from Lou must have really set her off! I hope Barney has found my MiniGen. Let's go up to the suite. I told him to meet us there."

Barney, the Green Man and Pouncer were waiting for them. "Nothing," stated Barney the moment they entered. "I could see nothing, and this wild animal didn't smell anything. But between *it* and Junior, I'm a nervous wreck. The one whistles when he shouldn't whistle, and the other one jumps all over the bed and drinks from the toilet!"

"Well, I wanted to be sure it wasn't under the covers, so I had to jump, and sniffing is thirsty work! You try going around sniffing everything, and see if you don't get thirsty!" explained Pouncer.

Uncle said that at least one more suspect was

eliminated, and then told the Green Man and Barney about their encounter with Tono and Tom. Beads of sweat broke out on Barney's bald head.

"That dame is out to get us," he declared. "I think that even if we didn't have anything to hide, even if there weren't any aliens or alien artifacts around here, she'd still want to get us for something! She just doesn't like us or UFO conventions!"

Chapter 9

Aliens and humans and Flixluns, oh my!

At one o'clock that afternoon, all other conference activities ceased for the opening of the exhibits. This was held in the Saguaro Hall on the main floor of the hotel. The exhibits were probably the most popular part of the convention. The Saguaro Hall was a large, open room, twice as big as big as a high school gymnasium. On this occasion it was filled with booths separated with three long aisles. People from all over the western United States had come here to sell their wares.

Most of the booths were small, consisting of a table with shelves or display boards behind it. One person, sometimes in costume, manned it. Several booths sold books, old and new, all having to do with UFOs. Another booth had DVDs, again having to do with UFOs. Not only were there documentaries, but a vast selection of movies based on the subject. One booth had nothing but posters of spaceships and alien beings, along with photos of various sightings. Another booth had UFO toys, such as ray guns, spaceships, action figures, light sabers, and even magnetic rocks said to be meteorites.

There were two large booths placed back-to-back. One sold costumes supposed to represent the various alien creatures described by James Cameron. There were blonde wigs and white robes, as described by Becky Moon. (They were very popular.) There were masks with bald heads and large, bulging eyes. Green amphibian outfits with frog-like masks were there too. Next to the white robes and blonde wigs in popularity were the Greys costumes. These were metallic-grey bodysuits topped with masks with large, black eyes and slits for nostrils. The other large booth contained an artist and his oil paintings – all, of course, of alien beings and/or spaceships. These were priced from $25 to $250 and were selling quickly.

The aisles were packed with convention attendees, many of them in costume. And aside from the official alien costumes, there were many Starwars outfits, including Luke Skywalker, Princess Leia and storm troopers. There were also blue angels with long blue robes and blue wings, robots of all descriptions, all sorts of bizarre creatures, including some creatures dressed in bodysuits with red and blue flames all over them. The most common costumes however, were the ones worn by Portia and Percy. It was obvious that Becky Moon's book had been a big hit with a good portion of the UFO crowd. There were also at least twelve other cats on silver leashes. Percy heard them described as Flixluns. When one of these pretend Flixluns got close to Pouncer, it would hiss and try to run away. Pouncer liked that and was always pulling at his leash to try and get close whenever he saw one. Portia would yank him back and tell him to quit drawing attention.

At one end of Saguaro Hall were half-a-dozen tables surrounded by chairs where exhibit attendees could rest themselves. Uncle and Barney, upon entering the exhibit area, had immediately seated themselves at one of these tables. There was nothing new or interesting to them at the many booths. They had seen it all before at many other conventions. It was all new to Portia, Pouncer, Percy, and the Green Man, however, and they excitedly visited every booth. As they progressed around the hall, constant stares were directed toward Portia and Pouncer. Portia ignored them, but Pouncer gloried in them. When he noticed a stare, he would go up to the person and jump on them and wait to be petted. Or he would wind his leash around their legs so they couldn't move, and therefore had to pay attention to him and praise what a fine looking Flixlun he was. Percy threatened to lock him in the room if he didn't quit getting tangled in people. He always claimed it was an accident.

If Pouncer didn't make Percy feel uneasy enough, he noticed two individuals who appeared to be following them. They were two middle-aged men of medium height. Both were overweight, with chubby round faces. Both wore yellow golf shirts and white pants, and both looked exactly alike, except for their hair. Both had slicked back black hair, except one's was parted on the left and the other in the middle.

"I'll bet those two are the Beamus twins," Percy whispered to Portia and the Green Man. "I think they're following us."

"I've noticed them, too," said Portia.

"Well, it doesn't matter," said the Green Man. "Let them follow us. It can't hurt."

"Maybe we ought to go back to the suite," suggested Percy. "It makes me nervous all the attention we're getting. Suppose somebody recognizes me. Suppose the Beamus twins have seen a poster of me. They've probably been all over Utah."

"Oh, don't worry," said the Green Man. "If they or anyone asks, I'll just insist you're my cousins. I'll say, of course, you look like a lot of boys your age. Let's just enjoy ourselves."

This did little to comfort Percy, because he knew, with his red hair and freckles, he didn't look a lot like other boys his age. In fact, he didn't know any other boys who looked like him. He didn't object to what the Green Man said; he just sighed, and they all went along looking in more booths. When they got to the end, they walked over and sat down with Uncle and Barney. The Beamus twins immediately came up to the table.

"Fine day for a convention," said the left-parted twin.

"Never seen a better day or a better convention,"

said the middle-parted twin.

"Yes, a very fine day and convention," agreed Uncle.

The twins stood there, looking first at Uncle, and then at Portia, as if they were watching a tennis match. When Uncle said no more, the left-parted twin said, "And who are your friends here?"

"Oh," said Uncle, acting surprised that he hadn't made introductions, but in reality hoping he wouldn't have to, "this is my nephew, Junior Green, and my niece and nephew, Portia and Percy Green. They're visiting me, and this is their first convention."

"I'm Casper," said the left-parted twin, "and this is my brother, Pollox. You can call him Polly; we all do."

"Delighted to meet you," said Pollox. He kissed Portia's hand and shook hands with the Green Man and Percy.

"You're from Aurora, Colorado, I see," said Casper. "Been there many times. Fine place, Aurora. You look very familiar," he added, staring at Portia. "Have we met before?"

"I'm sure we haven't," Portia said, smiling.

"You're so extraordinary-looking," continued Casper. "Once someone has met you, he is not likely to forget."

"You know how girls are," interjected the Green Man, "they all look alike."

"It's the costume," said Pollox. "She looks more

like the aliens Becky Moon describes in her book than any other girl at the convention. She looks veritably unearthly. That's why she looks familiar. If there's anyone here who could actually be an alien from Becky's book, it's Portia here."

"Yes, of course you're right," agreed Casper. "She does look alien."

"People tell her that all the time," said the Green Man.

"She doesn't get much sun, because she burns so easily," added Percy, nervously.

"Don't you think I look alien, too? Look at my tail and ears." whistled Pouncer, winding his leash around Casper's legs. Casper just untangled his legs and pushed Pouncer away, not understanding the whistling sounds.

"Why don't we buy you all lunch?" suggested Pollox. "We'd like to hear all about Aurora, and where Portia and Percy go to school, and what they're interested in."

"Sorry," interjected Barney, "but we've made plans for lunch; maybe some other time."

Casper and Pollox smiled and walked away. Without a word to one another, they walked to the elevator and returned to their room on the second floor. Once inside, and again without speaking, they filled the oversized Jacuzzi bathtub with cold water, stripped off their shirts and slacks, and climbed in. It should be noted that they weren't naked, but wore what could only be described as briefs and undershirts. I say could only be described, because they weren't briefs and undershirts. They were dressed in bright-yellow one-piece outfits that appeared to be made of shiny rubber.

"Ah," sighed Pollox, "that feels so good! This planet is hot enough without attending conventions in a place as hot as Phoenix! Why don't we just attend conventions in Wisconsin or Washington? It rains a lot in Washington. It's more like home in Washington."

"You know very well why we can't go back to Washington," growled Casper. "We crashed at Elk River, and it was only pure luck that we escaped the military! Besides, if we're ever going to get out of here, we'll need to stay close to Adam Green and his UFO conventions and conferences."

"I know you think he's an extraterrestrial, too, but I've seen no proof of that," said Pollox.

"That's true. From the first we've both felt there was something odd about him, something alien. But aside from that, I've got a hunch this convention is going to be different from all the others. First of all there is this rumor about an alien artifact. I think it's more than a rumor. Somebody here has got something that's real, and that something could just be what we need to get off this blazing ball that's only 93 million miles from its sun!"

102

"That could be, but who has it, and how are we going to get it?" questioned Pollox.

"It could only be with one of three people. My first guess is that Lou Lonewolf has it. He's the one who broke the rumor. I figure that either he got something from a crash site or somebody gave him something from a crash site. Sometime during the convention he's going to spring it on us all. His blog will go viral, and he'll be rich and famous.

"My second guess is that girl, Portia. Tell me, we've been on this planet for over thirty years, and have you ever seen a girl that looks quite like her? She doesn't have a wart, or a freckle, or a pimple, or a mole. Her skin is pure white and flawless. And that boy can't be her brother. I mean, he's light-skinned and all, but he's one big freckle! Then the other thing is, who is her uncle? None other than Adam Green, the guy we think is an extraterrestrial! That makes her one too.

"My third guess is Becky Moon."

"Becky Moon!" exclaimed Pollox. "She's just weird! I'll bet she just dreamed all that stuff in her book. Sure, we both know it sounds pretty close to some beings we've met in our galactic travels, but still, she's just too weird!"

"Listen," admonished Casper, "what if she's not weird? What if her book is true and she's got something, something she either stole off the spaceship or something she was given?"

"If that's so, why didn't she mention it in her book?" asked Pollox.

"I don't know, but there could be some very good reason. Maybe now that she's discovered there are people like you, people who think she's weird and don't believe her, she figures she has to reveal it! It's her ace card; her absolute proof."

"Okay, let's say you're right and one of those three has the artifact. What are we going to do about it?"

"We are going to search their rooms and steal it!" exclaimed Casper, slamming his fist into the water.

Meanwhile, back at the exhibits, Uncle was whispering, "Portia, the Beamus twins think you're an alien. They do this to everybody they meet who they suspect of being from another planet. They take them to lunch or supper and then start interrogating them, hoping to catch them in a lie, and then make them confess they're an alien. If they can, indeed, find somebody, then they can threaten them with exposure unless they get a ride back to their planet. So far they haven't found anybody they are convinced is a real alien."

Now, what Uncle, Percy, and the others didn't know was that they were being overheard as they sat there talking with Casper and Pollox. In a booth close to their table, but out of sight, Janet Tono and Tom Gerry had been listening. They couldn't hear the whisperings of Uncle, but they heard what Casper and Pollox said. In fact, they had been slinking from booth to booth, also following Portia through the entire exhibition. They now flowed out of the booth, down the aisles, and out into the hotel lobby. They seated themselves on a couch in a quiet corner and began to talk.

"I told you," hissed Tono, "that if we attended these things long enough we would turn up something. Now it looks like things are starting to come together. First, Lonewolf's blog hints at some big surprise, then this girl turns up. I think those two things can't be a coincidence. I think she has something to do with this alien artifact rumor. You could tell that even those idiot twins suspect she's an alien."

"But she's so young," said Tom. "She can't be more than thirteen or fourteen. Don't you think aliens would be older?"

"No, I don't. That's what they'd do," insisted Tono, her eyes getting blacker and beadier. "They'd send a young one to infiltrate the general population because no one would suspect her. She could gather all kinds of information on how to enslave our people, and we wouldn't even know what was happening!"

"I don't know," said Tom, shaking his massive head.

"I'll tell you something else," continued Tono. "I think that Adam Green isn't above suspicion either.

105

He's the one who brought the girl here; and, what's more, I've been doing some checking, and he was never born!"

"What!" exclaimed Tom in too loud a voice.

"Keep your voice down! I checked, and there's no birth certificate for him anywhere!"

"But that doesn't really mean anything. People are born at home or in a foreign country when their parents are on vacation. There are a lot of reasons why people don't have a birth certificate."

"Well, maybe," admitted Tono, "but don't you think there are a lot of unusual things going on around these conventions? I mean, there's just too much suspicious stuff to all be coincidences. And we can add this Becky Moon to the mix of odd stuff. She writes a book about aliens that look human, and then shows up at this convention at the same time as this –I can't think of a word for her –this girl, Portia."

"No, surely Becky Moon's not involved," sighed Tom, his big, gentle face lighting up. "Why she's just a lovely young woman who wrote a best-selling book. I'm sure the average person doesn't really believe it's true. But these UFO people will believe anything, and she's just here to make a few bucks. Surely you can't be suspicious of her! Someone so sweet!"

(Now, for those readers who can't already see it. Tom Gerry is in love with Becky Moon. He fell in love with her at first seeing her the previous day. He loved her with every bulging muscle in his oversized body!)

"I'm suspicious of everybody! I tell you, Tom, these conventions must all be shut down. They are nothing but a magnet for alien subversion and conspiracy!"

While this conversation was going on, Portia, Pouncer, and Percy, wanting to get away from the crowded exhibit hall, had wandered out of the hotel and into the swimming pool area, which was in an enclosure on the east side of the building. A wave of hot desert air enveloped them as they walked along the side of the pool, looking for a place to sit and rest their legs. All the lounges and chairs were taken except for some around a table shaded by a canopy. There was only one chair taken here, and it was occupied by Becky Moon. Not only was she alone, but she looked unhappy.

"Mind if we join you?" asked Percy, not really wanting to sit with her, but having no other choice.

"Okay, but please don't ask for my autograph," sighed Becky, not even looking up. "I'm tired of giving autographs and have told everybody to leave me alone for a while."

"We don't want autographs; we just want to sit," said Portia.

At the sound of Portia's voice, Becky looked up. "Oh, it's you. That's okay then. I somehow know you guys are different. You see, this is my first convention, and I don't really like being here. Not

107

counting you guys, there are only two kinds of people here -- ones who like my book and are nice, and ones who think my book is fiction, and that I'm a liar. I mean, after I wrote the book my publisher was really nice to me, and all the people I met at book signings were nice. You see, I never read what any of the critics said. But now I'm here some people even call me a phony and say my book can't be true. They say that no one has ever encountered nice, friendly extraterrestrials. What do you think?"

"Well, the truth is, we haven't read your book, and this is our first convention, too," admitted Portia.

"Oh," said Becky, "then how did you know to dress like that?"

"Our uncle Adam told us we should wear these for the convention," said Percy. "But we both hope to be able to read your book."

Percy leaned under the table and began unwinding Pouncer's leash from around the table leg. When that was done, Pouncer nearly pulled him over trying to get to the pool. "Get back here, Pouncer," Percy commanded. "Cats aren't allowed in the pool!"

"I'm hot," whistled Pouncer, "nobody will mind."

"They will mind, and we could get thrown out of the hotel! Just lay on the cool concrete under the table if you're hot."

"You talk to that cat like he understands every word you say," said Becky.

"Well, he's a pretty smart cat."

"The Flixluns on the Orion – that's the spaceship I was on – were pretty smart too," Becky said. "They could talk just like the aliens." She reached over and rubbed her fingers on Portia's sleeve, feeling her mushroom cloth robe. "Your cat's not a normal cat, and your robe feels very strange. You three are not like anybody else here. I know you're not from Atleaha --that's the planet my aliens are from – but you look a lot like them. Are you aliens from some other planet? I won't tell anyone if you are."

"We're not from another planet, but we are from an unusual place," replied Portia, not wanting to lie, and yet not wanting to be too specific. "That's all we can tell you."

"Okay," said Becky thoughtfully. "But do you believe my book is true? I mean, would you if you read it?"

"Sure, we'll believe whatever's in your book," said Percy. "Portia and I have seen so many strange things that people wouldn't believe if we told them, that it's easy to believe whatever's in your book. If we wrote a book, less people would believe us than believe you."

Percy felt sorry for Becky and wished he could help her, but he didn't know how. He was in pretty much the same situation with the Green Man, Uncle, and Barney and couldn't really add another problem to those already on his plate. He was glad Portia was here, otherwise he probably wouldn't help anyone and just ask the Green Man to take him back to Aurora.

"Look," said Becky, "over across the pool. There's Tom Gerry. I think he's been following me."

"Yeah, I think he's following us, too," observed Percy. "He and that dragon lady, Janet Tono, think we're spies or aliens or something."

"I met him and Tono when I first got here," said Becky. "I think he's nice, but I don't like her at all. I think she'd arrest me for something if she could."

"Me, too," added Portia.

"I'm hungry and thirsty," whistled Pouncer from under the table. "Let's go!"

"Well, we'd better go; Pouncer's thirsty," said Portia. "I hope things work out for you."

"Okay," said Becky, "but let me tell you this. Before this convention is over I'm going to prove to everyone that I'm not a fake!"

Chapter 10

*Becky Moon tells her story, her room is searched,
and everything goes black!*

Becky Moon was the featured speaker at that evening's banquet, and again the plan was for Pouncer, the Green Man, and Barney to search her room while she was speaking. Pouncer was excited about it, but he was also reluctant to miss out on a banquet. He envisioned missing out on all the fish and barbecued ribs he could eat, for since he'd been to this hotel, he never seemed to get enough to eat. Uncle told him that they wouldn't be serving any fish or barbecued ribs, and that cats weren't allowed in the banquet hall anyway. He pouted and said as hungry as he was, he didn't think he would be able to smell anything. After a consultation with Percy, Uncle called room service and had them bring up three pounds of hamburger, cooked rare. Pouncer whistled that he thought his nose would work very well after a dinner like that.

Uncle, Portia and Percy went down to the banquet, while Barney, the Green Man and Pouncer waited in the room for a half-hour to be sure Becky would be well into her talk before they began the search.

The Gila Room was even more crowded with people than it had been for breakfast. Lonewolf's blog about the mysterious announcement had made its anticipated impression, and those who couldn't get tickets were crowded around the four sets of double doors in the back of the banquet hall so that they could hear or perhaps even see what was going forward. The three squeezed their way in and made their way to a reserved table next to the podium. Percy noted that Janet Tono and Tom Gerry were seated at a table at the very back of the hall. This time, unlike breakfast, they weren't alone. Their table was full, because nobody wanted to miss a second of the convention, thinking an alien artifact could be revealed at any moment. So they were willing to endure sitting by Janet Tono.

Stuffed pork chops were served by waiters, who rapidly shimmered among the tables with armloads of plates and served everyone in an amazingly short period of time. Next dessert was served. It was something called a "snowball," and consisted of a large, round scoop of vanilla ice cream rolled in shredded coconut and served in a pool of chocolate sauce. Portia was in raptures over the snowball, and said she might consider staying in the Outworld if she could have snowballs every day.

While people were eating snowballs, Isaac Luboff, a well-known author of numerous books on

UFOs, introduced Becky. He said that her book had been criticized by many because her extraterrestrials were friendly. Although, he added, he had never encountered a story of friendly aliens, he didn't see why there couldn't be such things. He then turned the mike over to Becky.

"Not all of you have read my book," began Becky, looking down at Percy and Portia, "or know my history, so for those of you who know it all, forgive me if some of what I say isn't new to you. I live in a small town in southern Nevada called Gold Hill. It has one high school, and I am still a custodian there. Even though my book has been a success, I want to keep my job because of what happened in that school.

"But my encounter did not begin at the school. It began at Electric Lake, a lake not too far from town, and a lake famous for UFO sightings. It is called that because it's shaped like a lightning bolt. Since I was little, I've always heard stories of UFOs rising out of Electric Lake, and the townspeople believe that deep at the bottom of it is a UFO base.

"One Saturday, some friends and I were picnicking by the lake and wading in the shallow water. I felt something beneath my foot. It was just a slight bump or mound in the sandy bottom. I was curious, because on this beach there are not rocks or anything, just sand. I reached down and dug. Soon I uncovered a round, grey disk about four inches in diameter with three white dots on one side. It appeared to be made of some type of metal, and I thought it must be part of a kid's toy lost in the water. I don't know why, but I put it in my purse and forgot about it until Sunday, when I noticed it again. I took it to the sink and cleaned it with soap and water. It was then that I realized it wasn't a toy. It was something very strange, something very unusual. Even cleaned up it was still a dull grey, very smooth, perfectly-shaped, and very heavy for its size. I touched the white dots, even pushed them. They didn't seem to move or do anything. I put it back in my purse next to my cell phone intending to take it to school the next day and show it to Mr. Allred, the chemistry and physics teacher. I thought he might know what it was.

"My purse is small, and I carry it over my shoulder so I'll always have it with me no matter where I am in the school. I start work at 4:00, after school is out, and by that time I had again forgotten about the disk. By 9:30 I had worked my way to the gym and was sweeping the floor. It was dark outside, and I was the only one in the school. Suddenly, my whole body began to vibrate, as if I were a giant cell phone put on mute. Then I heard a low, soft hum that seemed to be coming from above. I looked up at the roof of the gym. It is made of metal, supported by large, metal beams.

"The hum grew no louder, but the ceiling became

114

kind of blurry, and a spaceship sank through it as if it were passing through a cloud. It didn't break anything. It just passed through the steel ceiling as if it weren't there! The ship was a dull, medium-grey, just like the disk. It was shaped like a football and filled the entire gym. On its bottom were two bright, white lights shaped like triangles. Along the middle of its sides were a continuous line of alternating red, green, and blue lights that flashed on and off. I backed against the wall, and as I did so I realized that the vibration I felt was coming from the disk in my purse. I took it out and held it in my hand. The vibration slowed until I could barely feel it.

"I wanted to run, but was so scared I couldn't move. As it settled on the gym floor, a hatch opened in the side of the ship, and three beings walked down a short ramp and toward me. There was a man and a woman. Both were tall, blonde, with green eyes and pale skin. The other was an animal that looked like a large house cat. It was yellow with black spots and a black tail and ears. They walked toward me, smiling. The woman held out her hand and told me, in perfect English, not to be afraid; they wouldn't harm me. She told me that the disk I was holding had signaled them.

"It turned out that the disk had some special purpose. They never told me what that was. It seems that it was lost when one of their ships crashed in Electric Lake many years ago, and they had been looking for it ever since. It seems that my pushing the white buttons while cleaning it, and placing it near my cell phone, had activated it, and they traced the signal back to me.

They said that as a reward for finding it, they wanted to take me for a ride in their spaceship and tell me about their planet and culture."

At this point in Becky's talk, the lights in the Gila Room went out, came on again, went out, came on, and then dimmed. Murmurs and exclamations ran though the hall. Becky stopped speaking and looked around her, wondering what was happening, and whether she should continue. As she was trying to decide, a hotel employee in a green blazer hurried into the hall and up to the podium. He whispered something to Becky, and she stepped aside.

"Ladies and gentlemen, we have just been informed by the National Weather Service that a massive sandstorm is approaching the Phoenix area. A huge wall of dust and sand is likely to hit the hotel soon. In the likelihood that the power should go out, our backup generator will take over, and so the lights should go out for no more than a minute or so. Please don't be alarmed, and just continue with your meeting. We do advise, however, that you stay inside the hotel until the storm is over. Thank you."

"So that means we could be in the dark for a bit," whispered Portia to Percy, "and I have to go to the bathroom. Maybe I'd better go right now."

"Good idea," said Percy. "There are restrooms out

116

in the hall just to the left."

Portia got up and quickly left just as Becky stepped in front of the microphone again. She seemed a little confused. "Where was I?" she said to no one in particular. "Should I continue, do you think?"

Scattered voices from across the hall shouted "Yes," and "Go on."

At this point, dear reader, I'm afraid we must leave the Gila Room to pursue other events in our own story and, sadly, leave out some of the juicer bits of Becky's story. You'll pardon me if I say that we must follow Portia into the Ladies' Room. You see, just as she exited the hall, someone else leaped from her chair next to the door and followed her.

"You stay here," hissed Janet Tono in Tom Gerry's ear. "I have a few questions for that Portia girl, and I want to talk to her while she's alone. You take notes if Moon says anything important while I'm gone." Before poor Tom could say a word, she was gone.

Portia had just come out of the bathroom stall when she saw Tono standing by the sinks. She stopped, startled at seeing this woman, not much taller than she but far broader, standing before her, glaring.

"Do you know who I am?" growled Tono, moving directly in front of her.

"Not really," answered Portia. "I remember your name from when we were introduced."

"I'm Janet Tono, a special agent for the

Department of Homeland Security." She flashed a badge at Portia.

"That sounds very important," said Portia. "Is there something wrong?"

"That remains to be seen. I have a few questions for you, and I need you to accompany me to my room." She glared even more fiercely at Portia.

"Oookay. Can I get my Uncle Green and Percy to come, too?"

"No, you can't. This will be a private interview with just the two of us. Now, if you will just come with me, this will be over in a few minutes. I'm sure you don't have anything to hide, do you?"

Well, of course, Portia had a great many things to hide, but she didn't want Tono to know that, so she didn't answer the question. Janet Tono gripped her elbow and led her out of the restroom and onto the elevator. Portia thought of slipping out of her grasp and running away, feeling very confident that Tono had no chance of catching her, but she decided against it. She thought it might end up causing more trouble, and Tono did say it would only take a few minutes.

They exited the elevator on the 9th floor, and, without letting go, Tono guided her into room 966. "Have a seat," she said with a forced smile. Portia sat on the sofa, and Tono began pacing back and forth in front of her.

"What is your name?" commenced Janet Tono.
"Portia."

"And your last name?"

Portia didn't have a last name. Most people in Aurora didn't have more than one name. She was, of course, Princess Portia, but princess wasn't her last name. She couldn't remember ever in her life telling an outright lie, but she felt trapped and a little desperate; and so she said, "Green."

"And where are you from?"

"Aurora."

"Now, tell me, Portia Green, from Aurora, Colorado, how long have you known Becky Moon?"

"I just met her today."

"Is that so. Did you attend Mr. Cameron's discussion of ufology this morning?"

"Yes."

"So you heard him describe one of the species of extraterrestrials called Nordics?"

Portia said, "Yes."

"Now, I know you were in Miss Moon's meeting just now, because I saw you there. You heard her describe the extraterrestrials she encountered. Did they or did they not match the ones described by Mr. Cameron as Nordics?"

"They sounded like the same sort of people," agreed Portia.

Tono stopped pacing and whirling around to face Portia, and, pointing a chubby finger at her, she snapped, "And how would you describe yourself?!"

Portia was taken aback and didn't quite

understand what she was driving at. "I don't know what you mean."

"You don't know what I mean? Come, girl, let's not play games. What do you look like?"

"Well, I'm thin and tall for my age, and I have blonde hair and green eyes. But can't you see that?"

"Of course, I can see that!" fumed Tono. "I can see that you look exactly like the Nordic aliens described by Cameron and Moon! And I mean exactly like!"

"But there are a lot of girls who look just like me that are at this convention!" pleaded Portia.

"Ah, there's where you're wrong! There are no girls that look *just* like you! There are girls who are dressed like you, girls with blonde hair and green eyes, but you're unique. It's as if they are all trying to imitate you!"

Portia didn't know what to say, and so she said nothing. She was becoming very nervous and scared. What if she slipped and said something she shouldn't? If Janet Tono found out who she truly was, then she'd find out about the Aurora Dome, and possibly the Green Man and Uncle. She didn't know much about the Outworld, but she knew enough to realize that it was essential that the Green Man and Uncle not be revealed as extraterrestrials, let alone that there was a place called Aurora that wasn't in Colorado! The Outworld must never know about the Netherworld!

"Now, I'll tell you something, young whatever-you-really-are. I've been going to these conventions for some time, and I've been suspicious all along that there's some alien activity going on at them. But there are just too many strange things going on at this one for me to just stand back and observe!

"This uncle of yours, Adam Green, do you know that he doesn't have a birth certificate?" (Portia didn't even know what a birth certificate was. Your birth was just recorded in a book when you were born in Aurora.) "Do you know he has to be much older than he looks? I won't go into how I know that, but let's get back to you. Becky Moon shows up at this convention describing an extraterrestrial being that looks just like you! You're here; your suspicious uncle sponsors the convention. Lou Lonewolf starts putting out rumors about an alien artifact. Maybe it's not an alien artifact that's going to be revealed, but an alien! Maybe it's you!" Tono's nose and cheeks turned a dull purple.

At this moment, when poor Portia was about to sink under the cushion of the couch in alarm, the lights went out. Janet Tono gave a screech, like the sound a toad would make upon having its foot stepped on. This Homeland Security agent was scared! She thought Portia had somehow caused the lights to go out. But moments later the lights came back on again, and she realized that the city power had gone out because of the storm, and the backup generator had come on. The look of relief that spread across her face was short-lived, however, for the lights began to slowly dim and then fade out again. The backup generator had failed!

Outside the hotel a massive wall of reddish-brown dust and sand had been making its way across the city. Power lines bent like bow strings and then snapped. Palm trees blew over, as if they had no roots. The full moon became a dark-red ball before it disappeared completely.

Let us now retrace our steps and go back to the time when Portia was making her way to the restroom. Becky, you'll remember, was relating how the aliens had taken her aboard their spaceship, and then had been interrupted by the announcement of the coming storm. After pausing and hesitating, she continued her story until the lights went out completely and the emergency generator came on. At this point she said, "I think I am going to discontinue my story, because this storm warning and the lights going out has made me nervous, and so, while the microphone still works, I have something very important to reveal. Something that isn't in my book."

It was at this moment that the light faded out for the second time; and the Gila Room was plunged into darkness, and the microphone went dead. Cries of alarm echoed through the room, and immediately faded as very dim lights went on above the exits. A flashlight appeared in the hall, and the hotel employee holding it entered.

"Ladies and Gentlemen!" he shouted. "I'm sorry to announce that our backup generator has malfunctioned. It is being worked on, and we hope to have it running soon. In the meantime, you're welcome to remain here, or, if you like, take the stairs to your rooms. However, emergency lights are only in the stairwells and halls. There are no room lights. Also be advised that the elevators aren't working."

What was Becky Moon going to say, everyone wondered? Was it something about the rumored alien artifact, or was it something else? Was it just some supplemental information she had left out of her book? Had her alien friends given her a souvenir? They would all just have to wonder until the lights came on again.

"Let's go to our room," whispered Uncle to Percy. "I've got a flashlight up there, and we need to see what's happened to Barney, Junior, and Pouncer."

"We have to find Portia first," said Percy. "Let's go to the ladies' room."

As Percy and Uncle made their way into the hall, they became part of a crowd of about half the audience, who were also leaving. They stood outside the restroom for several minutes, waiting. When Portia didn't come out, Percy opened the door several inches and called, "Portia, are you in there?"

When no one answered, he said, "Wait here. I'll go back to the table and see if we somehow missed her in the crowd."

Of course, she wasn't at the table, and so they decided she, too, was making her way to the room. They started up the stairwell. It took some time because Uncle tended to dawdle, and there were ten floors to climb.

Now, it should be noted that the Beamus twins both had small pen-like flashlights with them. They always carried these in their pockets, along with a few other emergency supplies, such as penknives, string, matches, compasses, water purifying tablets, and ten $100 bills each. After their narrow escape from the army, they never knew when they'd need to escape again.

"Did you hear what she said just before the lights when out?" whispered Casper to Pollox. "That she had something important to reveal, something not in her book!"

"Of course, I heard," replied Pollox. "She was talking about the alien artifact! What else could be so important? It has to be in her room. Let's get there and find it while she's still down here." He patted his shirt pocket. "With this universal key I designed, we can get into any room anywhere!"

Now there was someone else who had the same idea, and that someone was Lou Lonewolf. He started for Becky's room, too, but not knowing how he was going to get in. His only hope was that with the power out he might be able to force the door. He didn't even have a flashlight, but he was so obsessed with finding

124

the object, he was just going to search her room by touch and feel! This was his big chance, his big break to become the greatest, most famous UFO blogger in history!

It so happened that he entered the stairwell just a little after the Beamus twins and could dimly see them ahead of him. He knew their room was on the second floor (They always insisted on a room on the second floor, so they could leave quickly should circumstances require.), and so was surprised when they bypassed it and continued on up the stairs. It didn't take him long, however, to figure out what they were up to. Maybe, he thought, this is a good thing. They've got flashlights; they're always so sneaky that they probably have a key to the room. Maybe I can figure out a way to get the artifact away from them, even steal it, if necessary! (It had never occurred to Lou that the Beamus twins were aliens. They always seemed to him to look and act the same odd way as most UFO fans.)

We will leave the Beamus twins and Lou climbing the stairs and see what's happening with Becky Moon and the love-struck Tom Gerry. When the lights went out and the microphone went dead Becky just stood there at the podium, watching people leaving and people remaining at their tables. She didn't know what to do. Maybe, she thought, I'll just stay here until the power comes back. Then I can finish my talk. She leaned on the podium, peered over the top of it and waited.

Tom was in a similar quandary. He didn't know whether to wait for Janet Tono to return, go to his room and wait to hear from her, or go to her room. He also decided to stay where he was and, looking around, noticed that Becky was still standing at the podium. This, he decided, was his chance. He could go talk to her as a man and not an agent of the Department of Homeland Security.

"Are you all right, Miss Moon?" he asked, standing under the podium and looking up at her.

"Yes," she answered coldly, but not unkindly. She was in no mood to be questioned by some government agent.

"Good. I enjoyed your talk," continued Tom, understanding her chilly reply. "You've had a very exciting experience. I would like to have been there. I mean, not as an agent; just as a person like you. Just between you and me, I think Miss Tono takes these UFO threats too seriously."

"You do?" said Becky, relaxing her tone and manner. "I wish somebody had been there with me, too. It's just that so many people don't believe me. I mean, even some UFO people don't believe me because my aliens were nice. I keep thinking that you and Janet Tono are going to arrest me for something. If somebody else had been there, maybe everybody would believe me!"

"Well, don't you worry. I'll make sure nobody arrests you!" Tom knew he shouldn't say that, because he really couldn't guarantee it, but he couldn't help himself.

"Thank you!" sighed Becky. "That makes me feel so much better. I was wishing I hadn't come to this convention. It was my publisher's idea, and I do so want people to not only buy my book, but believe it!"

"I wish the lights would come back on," said Tom. "I'd like to buy you a big cold drink!"

Becky smiled and said, "I'd like that!"

Chapter 11

An alien artifact is stolen, or is it?

Percy and Uncle finally made it to their suite on the tenth floor. They entered to find Pouncer, the Green Man, and Barney, but not Portia.

"Where's Portia?" asked the Green Man.

"We don't know; we thought she'd be here by now," said Percy. "I guess we somehow got ahead of her."

"She went to the restroom, and we lost her when the lights went out," explained Uncle. "She'll probably be here any minute. Did you find my MiniGen?"

"No, it wasn't there," said Barney.

"Pouncer said it might have been there, but if it was it was taken away," added the Green Man.

"Yeah, I got this scent like it had been there in a dresser drawer; but it was real faint, so I'm not positive."

"We got back just before the lights went out," said Barney. "You know, I don't think this search thing is going to work, least not the way we're doing it. Young Pouncer, here, nearly tipped over the dresser trying to smell in the drawer. Luckily, I caught it. He drank from the toilet again and splashed water all over the floor. I had to clean that up. And he only *thinks* he smelled something! As for your nephew, here, when we came out of the room, he was nowhere in sight. What good is a lookout that's nowhere in sight?"

"I thought I heard something and went round the corner to see. Then I sort of forgot to come back promptly," explained the Green Man.

"You see what I mean!" moaned Barney. "We need a different approach to this searching thing!"

"Hey, how come all the lights went out anyway?" whistled Pouncer.

Percy explained, and then added what Becky Moon had said just before the generator failed. "So Pouncer could be right. Becky has the MiniGen. She probably hid it in her room and then took it with her down to her talk."

"If that's the case, what do we do now?" groaned Barney.

"The first thing we need to do is find Portia," said Percy, nervously. "She should be here by now. Something must have happened to her."

Everyone was silent. Finally, Uncle said that they shouldn't be alarmed yet, that any number of things could have detained her. Maybe she was just slow. He suggested that they just wait a little longer. Percy was already alarmed. He just had a feeling something had happened to her. He knew she wasn't slow. She was the fastest person Percy had ever known, but he had to admit that some unforeseen something could have

129

detained her; so he agreed that they should just sit and wait a little longer.

Meanwhile, back in Janet Tono's room it was pitch black. Stumbling and fumbling around, Janet found the doorknob and opened the door. The dim battery-operated light in the hall casts a yellow, sinister glow into the room. All Portia could see was the stubby outline of the Homeland Security agent standing in the doorway.

"You know," sneered Janet, "the backup generators in these hotels are checked regularly to ensure they're working. It's very strange and almost impossible for them to fail – that is, unless they're sabotaged for some reason. Maybe when you didn't return to your table your Uncle Adam knew something was wrong and arranged for the lights to go out! Or maybe Becky Moon realized that you were one of the aliens from the spaceship she was on and was about to reveal it. So Uncle Adam made the generator fail!"

"I'm no alien!" protested Portia. "I'm as much from this planet as you are! I've never seen Becky Moon before this convention, and I haven't even read her book! And Lou Lonewolf said there was a rumor about an alien artifact, not an alien person. If he were talking about me, wouldn't he have said an extraterrestrial being?"

"Mmm, there's something in that," said Tono,

more to herself than Portia. "Maybe all this is more complicated than I thought." Her beetle brow wrinkled, and her lips pursed together. "I see it all now! Adam Green is an agent, too, kind of like me, only he's a secret alien agent, sent to Earth to make sure no extraterrestrial being ever exposes his existence to the people of this planet until all is ready for the big invasion! He sponsors these conventions so he can keep tabs on all the other extraterrestrials. You're an alien agent, too, only your job is to gather information about the people of Earth and pass it along to Adam, who passes it along to the higher-ups! Now, as far as Becky Moon goes, she's not an E.T., but what she says in her book is true. She found that grey disk, and she met the people in the spaceship, but there's something she didn't put in her book. She stole something from that spaceship. Maybe it's one of those grey disks; maybe it's something else, but she's going to reveal it at this convention, and you and Adam have to get it back before she reveals all!"

"You're crazy!" shouted Portia. "First you said I was from the spaceship Becky was on! You're just making stuff up! If you don't let me go, Percy will find me, and he'll get me away from you!"

"Percy, that's the freckle-faced kid. He's going to take on the Department of Homeland Security, is he? Don't tell me he's an E.T., too. But hey, maybe he's in disguise. Yeah, maybe he's one of those Non-Greys made up to look like a kid! Adam said he was a

131

relative, like you. Good grief, how many aliens are in this hotel right now, I wonder!"

"You're letting your imagination run away with you," fumed Portia. "I'm an earth kid, Percy's an earth kid. Be reasonable!" (Portia didn't mention Adam, and she didn't let Tono know that there was an alien artifact or that Becky may have it. She kept silent about those things.)

"And what about this other guy, this Junior Green? He could be Adam's son," speculated Tono, "I wonder how he fits into all of this? He has to be an alien, too, and he's the weirdest of all. He gives me the creeps, the way he goes around like he hasn't a care in the world. He probably knows when the invasion will take place!

"I'll tell you what little missy. As soon as the lights come back on, or as soon as I can get hold of Tom Gerry, we're going to round up the bunch of you! We have a place for your kind; It's called Area 51. Once there, I'll guarantee you'll talk. Not only that, but nobody on this planet will ever see you again because you'll never leave Area 51!"

Meanwhile, the Beamus twins were walking down the hall of the 9th floor, gasping for breath and flashing their lights on each door, looking for room number 966. Several other people were in the hall, too, and so Lou Lonewolf wasn't noticed by Pollox and Casper. They soon found it and in a moment were

132

inside. Lou quickly slid up to the door and placed his foot against it so it didn't lock shut, but also let in a little of the dim yellow light from the hall. He placed his ear against it and listened.

"Where should we start?" wheezed Pollox.

"It doesn't matter," gulped Casper, "start anywhere."

Pollox sat on the bed. "I need to rest first! I haven't been so out of breath since that army corporal was chasing me through the woods at Elk River."

"We don't have time to rest! Becky could be on her way here at any moment!"

"What do you think we're looking for?" asked Pollox. "I mean, it would help if we had some idea."

Casper grabbed the opposite edge of the mattress and heaved it up. Pollox slid onto the floor. "Hey, what are you doing?" he complained. "She'll know somebody's been here!"

"Who cares? Just look everywhere, and make it fast!" commanded Casper.

Pollox stood up, rubbed his bum, and directed his light to the dresser against the far wall. He walked over to it, opened the top drawer, and began throwing things out. "I still don't know what we're looking for," he muttered.

"You'll know if you find it," explained Casper. "It will be something alien, something you haven't seen on this planet before. Just keep looking."

After searching through the bedding, Casper

went to the bathroom and opened the medicine cabinet. "Hey!" he exclaimed, "I think I found something!"

While this search was going forward, Lou Lonewolf was keeping his ear on the crack in the door and his eye on the door to the stairwell. (If somebody came by he'd pretend to be opening it.) He knew about Elk River because he'd reported on it, but wondered what Pollox meant by a corporal chasing him. He concluded that the twins were probably snooping around up there like he and many others had years ago. Suddenly, the stairwell door opened, and in the dim light of the exit sign Becky Moon and Tom Gerry stepped into the hall.

"Hey, you two, beat it!" hissed Lou through the crack in the door.

This was just at the instant when Casper found the *something* in the medicine cabinet. That *something* was a silver metal tube about seven inches long and three inches in diameter. Casper didn't have time to examine it, for the voice at the door made him nearly leap into the sink! He slipped the tube in his pocket and, pushing Pollox before him, stumbled and tumbled, the two of them, toward the door.

Meanwhile, Lou walked quickly away from the door and toward Becky and Tom, hoping to divert their attention long enough for the Beamus twins to get away. He knew where their room was and planned to confront them there as soon as he left Becky and

Tom.

"Thanks for escorting me to my room, Mr. Gerry," Becky said. She was feeling very comfortable with him now that she found he wasn't at all like Janet Tono. And, despite his size, he was really very nice.

"Oh, that's okay," shrugged Tom. "I've really got nothing to do until the lights come back on anyway." (This wasn't exactly true, for he knew that Tono had gone after that Portia girl, and he was a little worried about what happened. He could be in trouble for not finding her, and he was nervous about what Tono intended to do to the girl. If she detained her, and she wasn't an extraterrestrial, then Portia could sue them, and they'd both be in trouble. Every day he wished he'd been assigned to someone else. He could hardly stand Janet Tono, and this Homeland Security job had turned out to be something he didn't like, anyway.)

"Besides," he added, "a pretty girl shouldn't be walking around in the dark by herself, anyway."

"There you are," said Lou, stopping them in the hall before they got too close to the room. "I've been looking for you, Becky."

Becky just stared at him. She'd read his blog, and he hadn't exactly come out and accused her of making up the things in her book, but he also hadn't been supportive. At best he had said she put a new light on the UFO phenomenon by writing about a kind of encounter no one else had ever experienced. She wasn't sure what he meant by that.

135

Tom noted her coldness and said, "Hey, don't bother her right now. It's not a good time."

"No, no, I won't bother her," said Lou. "It's just that before the lights went out you said you had something important to reveal to everyone. I'd like to know what that was. Not just for me, but for everyone who reads my blog, for all those ufologists all over the world."

"I'd rather not say just now," replied Becky. "What I've got to say and reveal to everyone needs to be done in public."

"So, there is an alien artifact?" asked Lou. "You didn't come out and say you were going to show people something but, . . ."

"Hey, that's enough!" growled Tom, getting between Becky and Lou. "She doesn't want to talk to you, shove off!"

Lou turned and, without another word, walked down the hall. He accomplished what he had set out to do and more. He had allowed the Beamus twins to escape Becky's room without being seen, and he now was almost positive that there was an actual alien artifact, and that the twins had found it in Becky's room. Now all he needed to do was go to their room and confront them with what he knew. He might have to share the glory of revealing the first real alien artifact found on earth, but at least he wouldn't be just a spectator as Becky announced it to everybody! Because she now wouldn't have anything to reveal!

Becky and Tom walked down the hall to her room, and she slid her key card into the lock; the light flashed green, and she pushed the door open. From the emergency hall lights they both could see the room had been ransacked. Tom pushed past Becky and looked quickly around, hoping to catch the vandal in the act. All he did was trip over the mattress. Becky pushed the door wide open and hurried over to help him to his feet.

"Somebody's been searching your room!" exclaimed Tom. "I'll bet it was that blogger guy! I'll go nab him before he gets a chance to hide whatever he took!"

"Don't bother," said Becky, grabbing him by the arm. "If he's the one, he didn't get anything. There's nothing in here to steal. I thought this might happen, so I took precautions. I may not be able to prove my story about UFOs, but I can prove UFOs do exist!"

Meanwhile, up on the 10th floor, Percy, the Green Man, and Pouncer had just determined to go in search of Portia. The Green Man, using one of his MiniGens, conjured up a flashlight for himself and Percy, and they decided to go back to the Gila Room and see if Pouncer could trace her scent from there to wherever she went. They had reached the seventh floor when they caught up with Lou Lonewolf feeling his way in the dim light. He was startled and embarrassed to be found on a floor so far above his room, until he realized that Percy and Junior Green didn't know where his room was.

"Hi, Lou," said Percy, "where you going?"

"Well, uh, I was going back down to the lobby. I thought there might be more light down there."

"We're going to the Gila Room," explained the Green Man. "We've somehow misplaced Portia and thought she might have gone back there. You haven't seen her, have you?"

"No."

"You'd better walk along with us," added Percy. "Without a light, you could trip on these concrete stairs."

Lou Lonewolf didn't want their company because he was trailing the Beamus twins, whom he had just seen take the turn toward the sixth floor landing; but he didn't want to arouse suspicion, so he said, "Thanks."

On the sixth floor landing they caught up with the Beamus twins. Pollox had insisted that they stop to rest on each floor, even though Casper was dying to get to their room so they could see what was in the silver cylinder. He could see and feel it bulging out of his pocket and knew it was solid and heavy.

Pouncer went up to Casper and sniffed the bulge in his pocket. Then he went over to Percy and whistled, "He's got something in his pocket that came from Becky Moon's bathroom. I smelled it in there."

"What's he doing?" asked Casper nervously.

138

"Well, you see that collar?" explained the Green Man, not wanting the twins to know Pouncer could speak. "That collar is electronic, a special device I invented myself. It's experimental, of course, but what it does is transfer cat purring sounds into whistles that Percy and I can then interpret as language!"

"Really!" said Pollox, amazed.

"Really?" said Casper, not at all convinced by this explanation, and now very suspicious of who this Junior Green really was. Somehow that story about him visiting from Aurora, Colorado, had never rung true. Furthermore, there was something about him that made Casper think he wasn't of this world, something that made him think of the word *newcomer*. He suddenly suspected that what he had in his pocket had nothing to do with the cat's whistling. It was giving off a signal that Junior Green had somehow intercepted.

"So," asked Casper, "what did the cat say?"

"Well, of course, it's sort of an abbreviated thing, but he says that what you've got in your pocket belongs to Becky Moon."

Casper and Pollox were stunned. How could that cat or anyone know? Casper's newly formed suspicion was confirmed. This Junior Green is an alien! How else could he have known about the artifact coming from Becky's room? And, being an alien, he was their ticket home!

"But how could he possibly know that?"

139

exclaimed Pollox.

"He says," explained the Green Man, "that he smelled that smell on Becky earlier today."

Pollox looked at Casper, and Casper looked at Pollox, both wondering what they should say or do. But they weren't the only ones. Lou Lonewolf, standing behind the Green Man, knew what Casper had in his pocket, and he, too, was wondering what he should say or do. If he admitted to knowing anything, would that spoil his chances of getting the biggest scoop of the century? If he kept quiet, could that possibly give him an advantage later on? He decided to wait and see what happened next.

Casper's mind was racing. Whether the cat or Junior Green detected it didn't matter. What should he do? Should he act offended and deny the object belonged to Becky? Should he say the cat and Junior Green didn't know what they were talking about? If his suspicion was right, and this Junior Green was an alien, like them, then maybe he could be convinced to give them a ride back to their home planet. In the long run, it really didn't matter what was in the silver cylinder if they could only get home. He decided it was best to do what he could to become friends with Junior – oblige him, get on his good side. He glanced over at Pollox, and his expression told his brother to follow his lead.

"Well now, this is amazing," said Casper, pulling the cylinder from his pocket. "We found this on the

140

stairs just minutes ago. Of course, we didn't know who it belonged to, but we were taking it to the lost and found."

"Yes," agreed Pollox. "Whatever it is, we haven't opened it; it's probably valuable, and we want the owner to have it back. We're known for our honesty, just ask anyone."

"Ha, they stole it from Becky's room!" whistled Pouncer. "They're like us, they're searching for the MiniGen, too! Tell them to hand it over, Percy, or I'll make their pants into rags!"

"What did the cat say?" asked Casper, getting more nervous.

"Oh, he just said it was really shiny," replied Percy, not wanting to cause a scene, which repeating what Pouncer said would do.

"Yes," agreed the Green Man. "It is shiny. Rather a curious object, all-in-all, I would say."

The Beamus twins looked at one another again, as if to say, "See, he's an alien; he knows an alien artifact when he sees it, too."

Percy poked the Green Man in the ribs with his elbow. He had no idea what the silver cylinder was. Maybe what Becky was talking about wasn't the MinGen after all; maybe it was another alien artifact packed in a silver cylinder. But he didn't want the Green Man saying things like it was a curious object.

"I don't think it's anything special," observed Percy. "It's probably just some girl thing."

"Yes, of course, it's probably just some silly girl thing," agreed the Green Man, taking Percy's jab-in-the-ribs hint.

"You know what?" said Casper. "You two probably know Becky better than we do. Why don't you take this thing and give it back to her."

"Yes," agreed Pollox. "It will save us the trouble of taking it to lost and found or finding which room is Becky's."

Casper handed the cylinder to the Green Man, who ran his fingers over it and stared at it intently. He had never seen anything like it and couldn't imagine what it was. "Good idea. We'll be seeing her sometime soon, and we'll be sure to give it to her." He slid it into his shoulder bag, and there was a clinking sound as it hit one of the MiniGens.

The five of them continued down the stairs together. The Beamus twins became very jovial and complimented the Green Man often. They also said what a great man Adam Green was, and how the UFO world practically owned its existence to his conferences and conventions. Pouncer kept whistling rude remarks about them and saying how he'd like to send them in a boat over the Endless Falls.

While this was going on, Lou Lonewolf slowly kept easing into the background until he was in the section of stairs above them. He wanted to get out of sight but stay within hearing distance. He had decided it would be best to follow the silver cylinder, no matter who had it and keep record on his iPad of everything that happened. Then when the time came, when he knew exactly what was in the cylinder, and perhaps even its origin, he would immediately post it on his blog. If possible, he would even take a photo and post it, too!

Chapter 12

A rescue!

When they reached the lobby it was full of people milling about. Everyone was waiting for the storm to pass and the lights to come on, and there was really nothing to do until those things happened. The twins went one way, and Percy, the Green Man, and Pouncer hurried to the far end of the building. By the time Lou Lonewolf entered the lobby, everyone he was following was out of sight.

The three companions made their way to the Gila Room to start their search. The Green Man suggested they stop in some out-of-the-way spot and see what was in the silver cylinder. He was very curious, but Percy insisted that could wait. The main thing was to find Portia.

Pouncer sniffed the floor in front of the ladies' restroom. Yes, he whistled, he could detect her scent going in and coming out. (He said Portia's scent was very distinctive and reminded him of the wild strawberries that grew by Thistle Creek.) Straining his leash, he dragged them down the hall to the elevator and stopped.

"Well, that's it," declared the Green Man. "He's

144

lost the scent. She got on the elevator."

"He hasn't lost it," said Percy. "We'll go up the stairs and check at each elevator door, one floor at a time, until he picks up the scent again. If she got on the elevator, she had to get off somewhere!"

It was on the 9th floor that Pouncer found the scent again. He walked right up to the elevator door, smelled strawberries, and started on down the hall. Near the end was a room with its door open about twelve inches. Inside and against it was a chair. On this chair sat the square block form of Janet Tono. There was no mistaking who it was.

Pouncer strained at his leash, but Percy pulled him back. "Don't get too close!" he whispered.

"Why not?" asked the Green Man. "Let's just go up and demand to know if Portia's in there. Tono's got no right to detain her!"

"That's just it; maybe she has the right," explained Percy. "She's kind of like the police. Maybe she can detain Portia, and maybe she could detain us; if she wanted to! We especially don't want her to pay close attention to you!"

"Let me at her!" whistled Pouncer. "I'll make her think a Tasmanian devil has attacked her. I'll be so fast, she'll never know what hit her! And while I tear her clothes into rags, you get Portia out!"

"No! Wait a minute!" commanded Percy. "Before we do anything let's be sure Portia's still in there, and if anybody else is in there, too."

145

"And how do we do that?" asked the Green Man.

"With this," said Percy. He pulled up his sleeve to reveal the Oculus nesting in its bracelet. "Oculus, into that room," ordered Percy. The Oculus flew from the bracelet and zoomed through the gap in the door above Tono's head. Percy reeled with dizziness and held on to the Green Man's arm as his mind adjusted to seeing not only through his own eyes, but through the Oculus, too.

The room was dark, except for the dim light oozing through the doorway. Janet Tono sat with her arms folded, staring across the room. The Oculus turned in that direction. Seated on an overstuffed chair with her arms wrapped around her legs was Portia. She looked both scared and defiant. The Oculus turned slowly, looking for anyone else in the room. There was no one. Percy whispered his findings to the others. Then he turned his focus away from the Oculus and motioned his companions to walk farther down the hall.

He was at a loss to come up with a plan, but he knew he had to think of something. There was no way he was going to let Portia stay in that room with the horrible Tono. He desperately looked up and down the hall, trying to see or think of something. There were actually three lights in the hallway. One was the emergency light that hung in the center of the hallway and shown in both directions. The other two were the green lights that said "Exit" and hung above the

146

doorways to the stairwells at either end of the hall.

A plan suddenly dawned on him. It was a stupid plan, a crazy plan, but it was all he could think of. "Green Man, can you conjure up a flashlight that blinks red?" he asked in a whisper.

"Nothing easier." He pulled out a MiniGen, made some adjustments to it, and zapped one up. It immediately began blinking, sending a red shaft crazily in one direction after another. Percy clamped his hand over the lens and turned it off.

"We don't want it blinking yet!" he hissed. "Now, can you also somehow shoot out the emergency lights with your MiniGen?"

"That's easier than the flashlight!" grinned the Green Man. "I'll just adjust it so I get a thread-thin blue laser beam. That will pop the bulbs in any light!"

"Okay then, here's my plan, and it all depends on if Tono does what I think she will do. Pouncer, you sneak to the other end of the hall with this flashlight and put it down in the corner against the wall. When I wave my hand, you turn it on with your teeth and crouch down in the opposite corner. Green Man and I will sneak up as close as we can get to Tono's door. As soon as the red light goes on, you, Green Man, shoot out the emergency light and then the exit light. When everything goes dark, Janet Tono is bound to come out into the hall to see what's happened. If we're lucky, her curiosity will make her walk toward the red light. When she does, Green Man, you reach over my

147

head and hold her door wide open. As soon as she's down the hall a ways, I'll slip into the room, grab Portia, and we'll all run for the stairwell opposite our red light. Pouncer, you can see in the dark, so as soon as you see me with Portia, you head for the stairwell too. We won't use our flashlights. We don't want Tono to see what's going on, so we won't be able to see anything ourselves. We'll just run with our hands out, and when we get to the end wall, we'll feel for the other stairwell door. Hopefully we'll be in the stairwell and up to our room on the 10th floor before she knows what's happened!"

"Brilliant!" whispered the Green Man, "but shouldn't I do something else, like say, have the red flashlight levitate above the floor and twirl about a bit?"

Percy stared at him and then said, "We don't want her any more suspicious about what's going on in this hotel than she already is. A red blinking flashlight is one thing; a levitating flashlight is another!"

"Very well," said the Green Man, "but I still think a levitating flashlight would arouse her curiosity more than one just laying there on the floor."

Percy got a little dizzy and realized the Oculus was still in Tono's room. He focused on it, and then took one last look around before calling it back to its bracelet. Tono hadn't seen it; she was still sitting, brick-like, with her back to the door.

"Okay," whispered Percy, handing the flashlight

to Pouncer, "take this over to that far corner and wait for my signal."

Pouncer padded softly down the hall, so quietly that not even a mouse, if there had been one lurking, could have heard him. He slipped past Tono's room, stopped in the corner, placed the flashlight down, and looked at Percy. Percy could just make him out in the dim light. He motioned to the Green Man, and they both tip-toed to Tono's door. He waved his hand and Pouncer bit down on the flashlight. Red beams began dancing in the corner of the hall. Percy nodded toward the emergency light, and the Green Man aimed his MiniGen and fired. There were actually no noise or beams shooting out of the MiniGen; there was just a loud pop as the light bulb burst and the hall went dark. He then quickly turned and shot out the exit sign. The hall went completely black except for the red light display at the end of the hall.

"What the . . .!" exclaimed Janet Tono, as she hopped from her chair, knocked it to one side, and peered out the doorway. Only her head appeared, and Percy and the Green Man stood perfectly still and held their breath. Janet Tono was frightened. She didn't want to leave the room. She had a feeling something *alien* was going on. The only thing she could see was the dancing laser-like red beams at the end of the hall.

"What's happening?" asked Portia. Of course, she knew what was happening because she had seen the Oculus zoom into the room over Tono's head. She

149

knew that whatever was happening was caused by Percy, and he had a plan to rescue her. She readied herself for whatever came next.

"Don't you worry about it, girlie," snapped Tono.

"But the lights have gone out, and all I can see is some red glow."

"There's some red light flashing down the hall," said Tono, her voice trembling slightly.

Saying the first thing that came to her, and not knowing if it made any sense, Portia said the sort of thing she thought Percy would say. "Oh, it's probably one of those emergency buttons that you press to make the emergency light come back on."

"Emergency button?" said Tono.

"I think I've heard of them somewhere," ventured Portia.

"I've never heard of an emergency button." She looked nervously in the direction of Portia's voice, not knowing what to do, but thinking that maybe Portia was right. "Don't you move from there, missy," growled Tono, and she timidly walked into the hall. She looked directly at Percy and the Green Man but couldn't see them pressed against the wall. She then turned to the red light and walked cautiously toward it. Percy could track her movements by the way she blocked out the red beams. As soon as he figured she was almost to the light, he pushed on the door, the Green Man held it open, and he rushed in. He immediately collided with Portia, who was just about to rush out the door! Without saying a word, he grabbed her arm, turned, and started down the hall. The Green Man was on their heels.

Pouncer could see everything that was going on and was so interested in it all that he almost forgot that he was supposed to run. When he remembered he was to run, for reasons only known to the mountain lion mind, he ran between Janet Tono's legs instead of staying in the darkness unnoticed. Now it goes without saying that Janet Tono had stubby and stout legs, and there wasn't much space between them. When something fast and furry ran there, it rubbed hard on both sides and could hardly get through without wiggling and tremendous effort!

Janet Tono screamed in terror, pitched forward, rocked backward, and fell. There was a heavy thudding sound as she hit the floor, and by that time the three companions were in the stairwell, holding the door open. Pouncer swished through it, and it closed. Janet Tono was still laying on her back, stunned and wondering what had happened, and whether she dare move at all!

The four conspirators raced up the stairwell, down the hall of the 10th floor, and slammed the door of their room behind them. All this was done before a word was spoken.

"I knew you were coming," gasped Portia. "I saw the Oculus! How did you know where I was?"

"I followed your scent from the bathroom,"

151

whistled Pouncer. "Your scent is easy to follow, and I'm a good smeller!"

Portia grabbed him by the ears and kissed him on the forehead. "Thank you, my brave Pouncer!"

"What's happened?" asked Uncle. He and Barney had been seated on a couch, wondering where they were, when they suddenly burst through the door.

Percy caught his breath and then explained all. Rather than being happy, Uncle and Barney were alarmed. They said it was terrible – not terrible that Portia had been rescued, but terrible that she had been with Janet Tono. They reminded Percy that Tono was a government official and could cause big trouble for them. They said that she knew Portia was related to Uncle, and that she was staying in his room. She was likely to come up here any minute and arrest them all!

"We have to get her out of here," said Barney. "Does Tono know you three rescued her?"

"For all she knows, Portia just escaped," said Percy. "I mean, she may suspect something, but she didn't see a thing!"

"That's good, then," said Uncle. "Now all we have to do is hide Portia until we can figure out what to do next."

"But where?" asked the Green Man. "Maybe we could take her to another hotel. That's probably the best idea."

"No, we can't do that. There's a storm outside, and the power's out everywhere," Barney reminded

152

them.

"We have to hide her in another room in this hotel," reasoned Percy, "but how do we do that. They won't register anybody with all of the computers being down."

"Why don't we see if Becky Moon will hide me," suggested Portia.

"I don't know about that," said Barney, doubtfully. "I mean, she's nice enough, but she's kind of weird. I don't know how she would react to such a suggestion. She'd want to know why, and she might not like the idea and tell Tono."

"She doesn't like Tono any more than we do," said Percy, warming to Portia's suggestion."

"I agree," said Uncle. "She definitely doesn't like Janet Tono, and it would only be for another day. Portia would just have to stay out of sight until the convention is over; and if the lights don't come back on, the convention is already over. If that happens, I don't know what it will mean for our future, Barney, old boy. I suppose we'll have to refund at least some of the people's registration money, and we'll definitely go broke."

"Yeah, and things were just starting to look up, too, what with the rumors about an alien artifact, and the increase in registration. We could have made a little money or at least broke even!" groaned Barney.

Chapter 13

Alliances are made, and love blossoms even in the dark.

Meanwhile, back in Becky's room, Tom was helping her straighten things up and put the mattress back on the bed. Becky didn't ask him to leave, and Tom felt honored and privileged to be allowed to help. Girls never liked him much, and so he was even more enchanted with Becky when she allowed him to stick around.

"If you don't mind my asking, what did you mean when you said you'd taken precautions," he asked, as he put drawers back in the dresser. "You don't have to tell me if you don't want to."

"I'd like to tell you, but I don't know if I should. Since you work for Homeland Security and Janet Tono, it might be best if you didn't know too much. It might get you in trouble, and I don't want you to get in trouble."

"Yeah, I understand," said Tom. "You know, I wish I'd never taken this job. I was a deputy sheriff in a small town before I took it. I liked it there, but this job was a big promotion, so here I am. Now the only reason I'm glad I did is that I met you."

"Thanks for saying that," murmured Becky, smiling sweetly. She was like Tom in that men usually weren't interested in her. They always thought that she was kind of strange.

Becky had a little flashlight on her night stand, and using that and the light from the slightly opened door, she and Tom were able to straighten the room. They had just finished when there was a tapping at the door. Without thinking and before Tom could caution her to be careful, she opened it. There stood Percy, Portia, and Pouncer.

"Can we come in?" asked Percy, not realizing she wasn't alone.

Pouncer pushed his way in, as he always did, without being asked, and so Percy and Portia followed. They were shocked at seeing Tom standing there and didn't know what to do next. Should they turn around and leave, or make up some story about why they were there? Becky relieved them of the decision by saying very mildly, "Oh, Tom, do you know Percy and Portia, and their cat. I've forgotten his name. Anyway, this is Tom Gerry, a friend of mine."

Tom was surprised to see Portia since he knew that Tono had gone to interrogate her, but then he figured the conversation had been brief, and she had been satisfied with what Portia had to say. He decided not to mention anything about that.

"Yes, we've met," said Percy, dryly. "Maybe we'd better come back another time, when you're not busy."

"Oh, don't go," pleaded Becky. "We just got here a few minutes ago and discovered that someone had been searching my room. Everything was turned upside down. Tom helped me, and we just got things back together."

"Was anything taken?" asked Percy, knowing very well what was taken, and who had done it.

"I don't think so," said Becky. "It's too dark in here to tell for sure, but I don't think so." She didn't mention about the precautions she had taken.

"I think it was that blogger guy, Lou Lonewolf," Tom said. "I'd like to question him, but Becky said to let it go since nothing was taken. But he's got no right to search her room. I was just telling Becky that I think things are getting out of hand around here! There's too much crazy talk about alien stuff. Even my boss is getting crazy about it. I thought these conventions were just for having fun, and a place for people to sell their books and stuff."

Percy and Portia were surprised to hear Tom say this. They had thought he was just like Janet Tono. "Can I tell you something, just between us?" Percy asked Tom and Becky. "It's something we don't want anybody else to know, and I mean nobody!"

"Sure, go ahead," Tom said. "Becky and I can keep a secret." He hadn't really had a friend since he joined Homeland Security, and now he felt as if he were finally getting some, maybe even Percy and Portia.

"Janet Tono kidnapped me!" Portia blurted out. "She held me in her room and said I was an alien, and threatened to take me to a place where they keep aliens and never let me go! I'm not an alien! I come from this planet just like she does!"

Tom Gerry was surprised and stunned. He never imagined Janet Tono would go that far. He thought she was just going to talk to Portia, not detain her. That was illegal. Tono had definitely gone too far. He felt very uneasy and didn't know what to say or do. Maybe she had some special instructions from headquarters that he didn't know about. Still, he couldn't see how Portia could be somebody from outer space. She was very pretty, yes, but he didn't see how she could be an extraterrestrial!

"Well, I don't know what she's thinking!" exclaimed Tom. "I mean, how could she think you're an alien? You're just a girl! These last few days I think have driven her over the edge!"

"I've wondered, too, if you're an alien," said Becky, thoughtfully. "You do look a lot like the aliens I've written about in my book. But if you say you're from earth, I believe you. How did you get away from Tono?"

Portia explained how Percy had rescued her by luring Tono out of her room. She left out the part about the Oculus and the Green Man's conjured up red flashing light. She said that Barney and Uncle Green were worried that Tono might search their

157

room first since she was a relative. If she were found there it could cause trouble for them. She suggested that maybe Becky could hide her for a few days. Becky said she would be glad to, since she felt the same as they did about Tono. Tom would do anything to stay in Becky's good graces, and so he said he wouldn't say anything to Tono. It would be their secret. He felt uneasy about agreeing to this, but he adored Becky and disagreed with everything Tono was now doing. He also said he was sure Tono would be going to Barney and Uncle Green's room, and wasn't at all sure she wouldn't want to search Becky's room, too. He added that he'd volunteer to do that if the subject came up.

Becky smiled at Tom. "Thanks," she murmured. Then, turning to Portia, she added, "I'd like the company, and, besides, I'm for anyone who's against Janet Tono."

"Good," sighed Tom, nervously looking at his watch. "Listen, I'm wondering if Tono's been trying to find me. I'd better get to my room. If anything important happens, I'll call everybody."

"Then we can depend on you?" said Percy, holding out his hand.

"Sure!" grinned Tom, taking Percy's hand in his enormous mitt and shaking it vigorously.

Tom headed for the 9th floor, taking the stairwell, the one that didn't lead past Tono's room, and hoped she hadn't been looking for him. He was both a happy and unhappy man -- happy because he had made a favorable impression on Becky, and unhappy because he didn't know what he was going to do about Janet Tono. He needed his job and didn't want to lose it, at least before he could find another one. But he was going to do whatever he could to prevent her from hurting Becky or Portia. And he hoped he could do that by somehow tricking her without revealing his feelings for Becky, and without breaking his promise to Portia and Percy.

A few minutes later Percy and Pouncer made their way down the hall and toward the same stairwell that Tom had taken. Percy felt that, at least temporarily, Portia was safe, and Pouncer felt that he really badly needed a cheeseburger, or maybe a fish sandwich, or both. In his imagination he could smell the odor of hot, juicy beef. He could smell a whiff of lightly cooked fish. He could smell something else. It was a faint smell, an electric smell, a smell like the sun radiating off hot rusty cans in Pan Woods. He stopped abruptly, and Percy tripped over him.

"What are you doing?" complained Percy. "This is no time for playing around!"

"The MiniGen," whistled Pouncer. "I can smell the MiniGen. Just barely, but I can smell it."

"But we were just in Becky's room. Why didn't you smell it then?"

"Because it isn't in there. I already smelled that place. It's down this hall." He swung his head back

159

and forth and walked slowly along.

"Pouncer, we were down this hall earlier. Why didn't you smell it then?"

"We weren't down this part of the hall," whistled Pouncer. "We came from the other direction then." He stopped and sniffed a door next to the stairwell. "Here, it's in this room!"

"Are you sure?"

"If it's not in there, then you don't have to get me a cheeseburger and fish sandwich for breakfast!"

Percy knocked and waited. No one answered. He knocked louder. He was hoping no one would answer. If they did, he'd say he had the wrong room. No one answered. He tried the handle. It was locked. "Come on," he told Pouncer. "We'll have to get the Green Man to open it."

When they got to the room, the Green Man was asleep on the couch, and Uncle and Barney were dozing at the table. Percy noticed that at the center of the table stood the silver cylinder. Evidently the Green Man had showed it to Uncle and Barney. Percy wanted to ask about it, but this wasn't the time.

Uncle raised his head and said, "How'd it go?"

"Fine," replied Percy. "I told Becky what had happened, and since she doesn't like Janet Tono any more than we do, she was happy to help. The only thing is, Tom Gerry was in her room."

"Tom Gerry!" exclaimed Barney, sitting up straight in his chair. "He works for Tono! He'll run right to her and tell all. We'll all be in jail by daylight!"

"No, don't worry. He's on our side," explained Percy. "I think he kind of likes Becky, and when he heard what happened, he said Tono had gone too far, and he was willing to help us. So, everything's okay."

Percy then described what had happened on the way back, and that if Pouncer were right, the MiniGen was in a room just down the hall from Becky's. Relief spread over the faces of Uncle and Barney. "My boy," exclaimed Uncle, "if Pouncer is right, we may yet get through this convention without ending up in Area 51, or bankrupt, or both! Junior, wake up, we need your burglarizing talents!"

The Green Man, Pouncer, and Percy immediately headed down the stairs to the mystery room. "You sure no one's in there?" asked the Green Man, as he adjusted the MiniGen to settings that would open the door.

"Run if there is," whistled Pouncer, "but I don't think there is because I can't hear anything."

The Green Man pointed his MiniGen at the lock and pushed the button. There was a clicking sound, and the little green light on the lock flashed on. Percy pushed down the handle, and the door opened. He shined his flashlight around. The room was empty. The closet was open, and nothing was in it. No suitcase rested on the caddy. There was nothing in the room to indicate that anyone was staying there.

"It looks like no one has rented this place,"

observed the Green Man, "and yet Uncle said that after Lou's blog about the alien artifact all the rooms in the hotel were booked."

"Yeah," said Percy, "this is weird. Well, at least we won't have to worry about someone surprising us. Pouncer, sniff it out."

Pouncer zigzagged around the room like a bloodhound, sniffing in the closet, in the bathroom (stopping, of course, to take a drink from the toilet), and under the bed. He then jumped on the bed and sniffed around the pillows. Percy was just thinking he'd made a mistake when Pouncer sniffed the lamp on the night stand and whistled, "It's under the lampshade."

Percy shined his flashlight over the top of the lampshade. There, suspended by two rubber bands, was the MiniGen. He unfastened it and slipped it in his robe pocket.

"Well, I say that was a pretty clever place to hide it," observed the Green Man. "I would have put it under the mattress."

"Let's get out of here, just in case whoever put it there decides to come back," urged Percy.

Back in the 10th floor suite, Percy proudly handed it to Uncle, who sighed with relief. "Well, Junior was certainly right, young man, when he said you could help us! If it hadn't been for you, things could have turned out really bad!"

"Hey," protested Pouncer, "I'm the one who found it, and Percy promised me a cheeseburger and a fish sandwich."

"We'll get you both and more," Uncle assured him, after hearing Percy's translation. "The thing is, we can't do it until the power comes back on, so you'll have to wait."

"But I'm hungry now!" complained Pouncer. "Green Man can make 'em for me!"

"Here," said Percy, "here's a bag of Cheetos. Eat them. That should do you until things calm down."

Pouncer slit the bag open with one claw and devoured the contents within less than a minute. He looked up and grinned, his whiskers covered in orange powder.

Uncle sat at the table and examined his MiniGen. A spiral crack wound around it. "Look at this," he said, holding it up for the Green Man to see. "The crack is longer since I last saw it. It will probably never work at all again."

"Don't worry, Uncle. I"ll keep the broken one, and you can have one of my extra ones whenever you want it," the Green Man assured him. "I always carry a few extras, just in case."

Percy sat on the couch next to the Green Man as Uncle said, "Thank you. It's odd, though, the way we found it. We thought it would be in a room rented by one of the convention people, and instead, it was in an unrented room. How strange is that? Who would put

163

it in an unrented room? I mean, the room would at some point be rented, and then someone would probably find it. It doesn't make sense."

Barney, who had been beaming since the recovery of the MiniGen, suddenly looked worried. "Yeah," he agreed. "We thought Becky Moon had it. It doesn't make sense. Maybe it's a trap. Maybe someone wanted us to find it. Maybe there were cameras hidden in the room, and now they'll know it belongs to us! Probably Janet Tono set the whole thing up!"

"I don't see how that could be," said Percy, yawning. "We have a list of the only people who could have stolen it, and Tono isn't on it. How would she know anything?"

"Well," said Uncle, also yawning, "it will have to remain a mystery for now. Let's get some sleep. I'm too tired to even think anymore."

Chapter 14

Janet Tono rages and threatens.

A ringing noise woke Uncle. He rolled over and picked up the phone on his night stand. It was the hotel desk, wondering if the convention were going forward as planned. They said people had been asking. He picked up his watch and stared at it for a moment. It was 7:15 am. Brilliant sunshine was blasting through the window across the room. He asked if the power were on and was told it came on at 5:30. "Yes," he said, "tell everyone the convention will continue as planned."

This was the last day of the convention, and the first meeting of the day was to begin at 9:30. Steve Woods was to give a talk called "Area 51: New Revelations on the Secret Government Facility." After that there were two discussion groups, one on the Kingman Crash, and one on UFO's use of drones. Also on the agenda was Jake Noory's panel discussion on Roswell. After those, at noon, Becky Moon was to have a book signing in the exhibits hall. And everyone hoped she would include the announcement everyone hoped to have heard the day before. The exhibits would then close at 3:00.

Uncle got out of bed and called Steve Woods to remind him he was to speak at 9:30. He also called the convention registration desk to make sure the word got out that everything was back to normal. He then woke the others. While they were all getting ready for the day, there was a loud knock at the door. Everyone knew who it was.

Uncle immediately went to the table, picked up the silver cylinder and slipped it into the Green Man's shoulder bag. He thought it best if Tono didn't see it, even though she knew nothing about it. He whispered to the Green Man to keep it there. It was then that Percy realized in all the excitement of the night before he had forgotten to ask what it was. There was no time for that now, however, for the knock was impatiently repeated.

Uncle opened the door. A red-faced Janet Tono stood there, with Tom Gerry meekly standing behind her. "We're here to speak with your niece, Portia Green," growled Tono.

"Do come in," said Uncle, with a smile as he stepped aside. "I'm sorry to say she isn't here, however."

Tono and Tom walked in and stared around the suite. "You won't mind if we look in the bedrooms!" stated Tono.

"Of course not. We always want to cooperate with Homeland Security, but what's this all about?" asked Uncle. "Why do you want her?"

"It's Homeland Security business, but I'll just say that I was questioning her about certain things last night when I was attacked in the hall outside my room, and she fled away with several other people or things!" She glared down at Pouncer, who whistled, "You can't prove I did anything!" (Of course, she had no idea what he was saying.)

She and Tom walked through both bedrooms and even looked under the beds. "Where is she then?" demanded Tono.

"Percy said there was a bunch of kids having a party in the exhibit hall last night after the lights went out," explained Uncle. "We assumed she just stayed there all night. You know how kids are. They're always staying up all night. Why don't you wait here. She'll probably be back any minute."

"Yeah, you know how kids are," added the Green Man.

Tono swung around to face the Green Man. "How could she be at a party when I had her detained last night, and then she escaped?" she demanded.

"Maybe she went to the party after she escaped," suggested the Green Man.

Janet Tono's face changed from red to purple. "You're all toying with me!" she shouted. "You all know where she is because I'm positive you attacked me and rescued her. I know she's an alien, and some of the rest of you are probably aliens, too! What's more, I know there's an alien artifact in this hotel

167

someplace that can prove both things, because the alien artifact belongs to her or one of you! I'll find that girl and arrest her; then I'll make her talk, and when I do I'll know where the artifact is. Then I'll know who's who, and you'll all be arrested, and these subversive conventions will be closed down for good! There will be charges of consorting with aliens and planning for the destruction of the government! Mark my words!" She stormed out of the room and slammed the door, almost before Tom could get out.

"We'd better check on Portia and Becky," said Percy. "We'll need to figure out a new plan. Tono might be coming to their room next."

Meanwhile. . . "Janet," said Tom, as they walked in the hall, "calm down. We have to be careful. These people have constitutional rights. We can't just arrest people, or even accuse them with no proof."

"You don't know what I can do, Gerry. I'm in charge here, and you just do what I order! And you can start doing what I order by explaining where you were last night. If you'd been with me, I wouldn't have been attacked! You just showed up at my door this morning! After that attack, I wasn't about to go wandering around in the dark looking for you!"

"I wasn't anywhere," lied Tom. "After the lights went out, and you didn't come back to the Gila Room, I figured you probably just talked to the girl in the hallway and then went to your room. With the storm

168

raging and no lights, I figured there was nothing to do until morning, and so I went to my room."

"From now on," insisted Tono, "you keep in touch with me, no matter what the lights or storms do! Now, let's go talk to that blogger fellow, Lou Lonewolf. He's the one who started all this stuff about an alien artifact. I think it's time we got tough with him. He knows more than he's saying, and I'm going to find out what it is."

"Why don't I look around for Portia while you do that?" suggested Tom, wanting very badly to see Becky and tell her that Tono had really slipped into insanity this morning. He was also afraid that Portia would be found in her room, and the last thing he wanted was for Becky to get in trouble, too.

"No, you stay with me. I don't want to take a chance on getting attacked again. We'll go to the exhibit hall and find the girl later. She's got to be in the hotel somewhere!"

"So, what exactly happened last night?"

"All you need to know is that I was outside my room, and suddenly something flipped me off my feet, and I landed hard on the floor. I heard the sound of running feet, and when I recovered myself, that Portia girl was gone! I think that Percy boy and his cat had something to do with it. But never mind that now. Those Greens are going to pay for all the trouble they've caused me! But now let's go talk to Lonewolf."

Lou Lonewolf's room was on the 5th floor, and it was still early enough that most people hadn't left their rooms, especially since many had gotten little sleep. So Lou was still in bed as Tono and Tom approached his room. He had gotten the call indicating the convention was still on and was laying there thinking about what he should do. He knew that Junior Green and Percy had taken the silver cylinder from the Beamus Twins, and he had lost them in the lobby. What, he asked himself, had then happened to it? Did they keep it or give it to somebody? If they gave it to somebody, who? The answer was simple. If they gave it to somebody, that somebody would be Adam Green! Yes, of course, they would give it to Adam. He was related to them, and he was in charge of the convention! Adam and Barney were the ones who had first mentioned an alien artifact to him. But then, how did Becky Moon get it? Did she steal it? This was all confusing and didn't make sense. And now that Adam had it, if he did, what would he do with it – announce it today in front of everybody at the convention? Of course! This was the last day of the convention. If it were going to be revealed, it had to be today!

There was a great mystery behind this whole thing, and Lou wished he had the story behind the story. Where did the artifact come from? How did Becky get it? He wished he knew. He wished he could be the one to announce its existence at the convention,

170

and at the same moment publish it on his blog, with photos! He didn't see how that was possible now. Now he would just have to sit in the audience like everybody else, and then write the story based upon whatever Adam chose to say.

There was a knock at the door. Lou got up and trotted over to open it in his pajamas. "We need to talk to you, Lonewolf," growled Janet Tono.

Without a word Lou stood back and waved them into the room. He was always willing to talk. That's what a reporter did, talk, and then listen.

"We think that there's something going on around here that may be a national security risk, and you may be involved," stated Tono. The color of her face had subsided from purple to red, and now to an uneven pink.

"A national security risk? What kind of a risk?" asked Lou, thinking he may be getting a story he hadn't planned on.

"Never mind what kind of a risk," snapped Tono. "We need to know two things from you. First, what is the source of this rumor you published on your blog, the one about the alien artifact? And, second, what do you know about this girl, Portia Green, and her whereabouts?"

Lou politely reminded her that a reporter couldn't be forced to reveal his sources. But this didn't satisfy her. She asked him if he'd like to spend some time in jail while he thought about revealing his sources. The one thing that Lou Lonewolf had always longed for was a blog report that would make him famous, one with a readership that was so vast that he could really make money off it, and be known worldwide as the place to go for the latest UFO information. He despised Janet Tono, but the thought of going to jail scared him.

"I might be willing to give you some information," ventured Lou, "if I got something in return. Let's say for what I know, you give me the inside scoop on the whole story, including what happens today. That means I get to report everything on my blog before any other reporters get to."

Tono looked at him suspiciously. She was totally focused on her job and her role in keeping America safe, but she *did* like the idea of becoming famous all over the Internet for seizing the first ever alien artifact and maybe even the first alien. Yes, she could let Lonewolf publish something. "You can't report anything that might compromise national security."

"No, I wouldn't want to do that," said Lou.

"Anything I uncover about aliens you can't print unless I approve it. And you have to use my name as the agent responsible. Agreed?"

"Agreed," said Lou.

"Okay, what do you know?"

"Well, first, about this girl, Portia. I've been following these conventions around for years; in fact, since Adam and Barney started them. They were sort of a fun breakout from the more serious UFO conferences. I got to know Adam Green pretty well, and I never heard him mention any family members, until the day before yesterday when Portia, Percy, and Junior Green showed up. Now, Junior looks quite a bit like Adam, so maybe they're related, but I can't believe Portia and Percy are any relation. You've seen them. Percy's just some freckle-faced kid, but Portia's different. I mean, she's *different*!" Janet Tono nodded her head in agreement.

"She's almost too perfect to be human, and she looks just like those Nordic E.T.s that have been described so many times." Lou paused. He was feeling a little guilty about admitting these things to Tono, for he liked Portia and Percy, but he liked getting a great story for this blog better!

"In the five established categories of extraterrestrials, I've never seen anybody who meets the description more closely," Lou continued. "And another thing, why did these three show up so suddenly at Adam Green's door? He said they were just visiting and wanted to see a UFO convention. I don't believe it! I think they were unexpected and came because of some kind of emergency. I think that emergency was something to do with an alien artifact!"

"So, you think Portia is a Nordic E.T. and has the artifact?" asked Tom in disbelief. "I don't believe it! If she's an alien, why would she be around here, and

173

why would she be looking for an alien artifact?"

"Those are just the same things I suspect," declared Tono.

"She didn't tell me," said Lou. "Adam and Barney told me! I mean they told me there were rumors going around the convention about an alien artifact. That's where I first heard about it. They didn't tell anything about Portia. Then last night I saw something that kind of put all the puzzle pieces together." He paused again. It occurred to him that maybe he shouldn't tell Tono everything he knew. Maybe he'd better keep something to himself. It might come in handy later if he left the Beamus twins out of his story.

"After the lights went out, I was headed for my room when I noticed Percy, Junior, and that weird cat of theirs in the stairway ahead of me. I decided to follow them. Anyway, to make the story short, I saw them come out of Becky Moon's room with a silver cylinder. I couldn't see it clearly, but it appeared to be about eight or ten inches long and two or three inches in diameter. I followed them; they went back to the lobby, and I lost them in the crowd. Now, I don't know what the cylinder is or what's in it, but the whole thing looked very suspicious. Was it the alien artifact? I don't know, but I think it could be. Furthermore, what was it doing in Becky's room? How did she get it, and how did they know where to find it?"

Tom Gerry was shocked. He had been with

Becky when they found her room turned up-side-down. He saw Lou and thought he had searched the room. Becky said nothing was missing. Surely if the alien artifact was missing, she would have known it. Somebody was lying, and he didn't believe it was Becky.

"We're going back to Adam's room," growled Tono. "Lonewolf, don't leave the hotel. I'll let you know about everything that happens, as long as it doesn't jeopardize national security."

"But can't I go with you?" pleaded Lou.

"No, you can only join us when I say. I'll let you know when. Also, for now it will be best if nobody knows what you've told us," Tono added, as she and Tom walked away.

Lou wasn't about to be bossed around by Tono, at least not if he could get away with it. He quickly threw on his clothes and followed them at a safe distance.

Chapter 15

The silver cylinder is revealed!

$\mathbf{T}$ono, followed by Tom, followed by Lou, marched up to Adam and Barney's room and pounded on the door. Adam opened it, and Tono immediately demanded to see Junior Green. Adam stated that he wasn't there, and, without asking, Tono pushed her way in, sweeping Tom and Lou along with her and searched the room. Barney didn't object. He simply explained that he thought Junior, Percy, and Pouncer went down to the exhibit hall to find Portia.

"Is there something we can help you with?" asked Adam.

"No," snapped Tono, and trotted out of the room.

They went directly to the exhibit hall. It was crowded with people who were killing time until 9:30, when they could go to one of the various talks being held.

"We'd better split up and look for them, don't you think?" suggested Tom, anxious to get away from her and Lou and go to Becky's room.

Tono hesitated. She was still nervous about being alone since Pouncer had tripped her, but she was anxious to find Junior Green, and she knew the chances increased if they split up, and she did have Lou tagging along. "Yes, let's split up. We'll meet out in the lobby once we've found him. And bring the others, too, if they're with him."

The moment Tom was out of her sight, he rushed for the elevator and went to Becky's room. When he knocked on the door, the Green Man and Pouncer hid in the shower, and Percy and Portia in the closet. Becky called them from their hiding places when she saw it was Tom.

"I can only stay a second," he explained. "Tono is on the warpath. She's down in the exhibits looking for you guys, especially you, Junior. Lou Lonewolf told her that you and Percy stole a silver cylinder from this room, and she thinks it's the alien artifact!" He took a deep breath and then said, "Becky, you told me nothing was stolen from this room!" He was disappointed in her.

"I didn't know that was stolen," Becky protested. "Besides, it's nothing important. That is, nothing important to anyone else. It's just something personal, not an alien artifact!"

"So, it's not the alien artifact everyone's looking for and talking about?" asked Tom.

"No, that's not it."

Tom looked at her with a puzzled and confused stare. "I don't know what's going on, but I've got to get back. You guys can't stay here; she'll be coming here next. You'd better leave the hotel right away. I'll tell you what; go to the hotel next door, the Red Mesa. I'll meet you in the lobby there about 5:00. We'll decide what to do next."

"No," said Becky. "I've got a book signing at noon. Tono can't connect me to anything; at least, not now," Becky added enigmatically.

"Well, then," said Tom, halfway out the door, "you all can just go to the book signing, or whatever, I guess." He slammed the door and was gone. Becky could see he was mad at her, and that made her sad.

"Becky," said Percy, suddenly having an insight into what had happened to Uncle's MiniGen, "did you steal something from Adam's room – something that you knew was an alien artifact? You can tell us because we already found it. Pouncer and I found it in the room just down the hall. You hid it there, right?"

Becky hung her head. "When I saw it in Adam's bathroom, I knew it was extraterrestrial because I'd seen something a little bit like it on the spaceship I visited. On the spaceship what I saw was a long, slender crystal that had facets on it's sides and a metal cap on one end. It looked very similar to what you call the MiniGen. How Adam and Barney got it, I don't know and didn't care, but I knew it was alien, and it was a chance for me to prove myself--prove I wasn't lying. After my book was published, and I came here and discovered how many people thought I was lying, I've been hoping for a way to prove what I wrote was true. I thought that thing was my chance. I was about

178

to tell everyone that I would reveal an alien artifact today at the book signing, but then the lights went out."

"Did you think about the trouble you'd put Adam and Barney in if it were discovered the artifact came from them?" asked Portia.

"Let alone the trouble you'd be in with Janet Tono, when she found you had it," added Percy. "She'd make you tell where it came from; then we'd all be in trouble."

"I didn't think about anything," sighed Becky. "I just thought about me and took it."

"I've got a splendid idea," said the Green Man. "Why don't I just transport us all somewhere else? Somewhere where Janet Tono can't ever go!"

Becky looked shocked. "Transport us somewhere? Then that means you're all really aliens! I mean, I thought Portia was, but then she said she wasn't. Being aliens gives you special powers. That must be how you discovered the artifact in my other room. You see, I rented another room just to hide it, because I thought if the word got out, somebody might search my room, and I was right. It was searched!"

"Well," said Percy, "actually it was Pouncer who found it, and he's not an alien, and neither am I or Portia. Look, I'm going to tell you something, but you can't tell anyone else, and you can't write it in a book. Adam and Junior are from another planet. Junior will be gone soon, but Adam wants to stay here and continue making a living with these conventions. We can't let Janet Tono know about him or Junior. Do you see what I mean?"

"Yes," agreed Becky. "I won't tell anyone about any of you, but I want you to know that I'm not lying about what happened to me!"

"We believe you," declared Portia.

"Listen, I just thought of something," said Percy. "Since we have to get out of here, why don't we go to Becky's other room. Tono can't find us there, and we can decide what to do next."

"I could easily transport us to Aurora," suggested the Green Man.

"Let's go someplace where there is lots to eat," whistled Pouncer. "I'm starved!"

Percy ignored this, and they all slipped down the hall and into Becky's other room.

"My book is a bestseller, even though some people don't believe it. That's why I have plenty of money and was able to rent two rooms. I'm really sorry about stealing that crystal thing." She looked at her watch. "It's 9:30. Steve Woods will be starting his talk on Area 51. That means I'll have to stay here for two-and-a-half hours, 'til the book signing starts. Come to think of it, why should I stay here at all? Janet Tono can search me and my room, and she won't find anything. What can she do?"

"There's the silver cylinder. She's after it, and she

knows it was in your room. You don't want her questioning you about that," warned Percy. "By the way, what is it?"

"It's like nothing I've ever seen before, and I've been to twelve worlds!" stated the Green Man.

"It stinks!" whistled Pouncer.

The Green Man drew it from his shoulder bag and handed it to Percy. It was heavy, shiny and cold. Portia peered over his shoulder. Percy examined it and noticed a slight lip on the edge of one end. He gave it a half-twist, and it opened.

Percy laughed. "This is what Janet Tono is after! This is what she thinks is an alien artifact!"

"I don't want to give it to her," Becky said. "It has special value to me."

Portia took it from Percy and caressed it in her hands. "It's wonderful," she sighed.

"It stinks," repeated Pouncer.

"I guess I should just give it to her, and then maybe she'd leave us all alone," murmured Becky.

"Yeah, she probably would, for now," mused Percy, "but she'd still be hunting aliens and bothering Uncle Adam. What we need to do is make her look like such an idiot that she'll never come back to one of these conventions again."

"Why don't I transport her to another planet," suggested the Green Man. "Planet 1200PM has creatures on it that look a lot like her, only they have two heads, four arms and four legs. They roll

181

everywhere they go. They'd probably think she was one of them who had lost some body parts!" He smiled one of his winning smiles.

"You've been to so many planets," sighed Becky. "You've probably seen all sorts of being like we talk about at these conventions."

"Yes, I've seen things that would amaze you, but I've never seen anything like Greys or amphibians or lizard men. I think that's rot. All the really intelligent beings I've seen are some slight variation on me and you. I mean, there are other creatures more weird than any on this planet, and some are quite smart, but none that are smart enough to build and fly spaceships. Only people can do that."

Percy was pacing the room in a whirlwind sort of way, thinking, as he often did when under pressure. He had helped solve a number of problems, but some still remained. He didn't see how he could force Uncle to leave if he didn't want to. That was an unsolvable problem. He couldn't see that Lou Lonewolf was a serious threat, so he would ignore that. The Beamus twins were still a problem, and he hadn't yet figured out how to solve that. The main thing left was to figure out what to do about Janet Tono. She was after Portia because she had convinced herself she was an extraterrestrial. She was after the silver cylinder because she thought it was the alien artifact. She obviously thought that if she could confiscate the cylinder and capture Portia, she would be able to shut

182

down UFO conventions, and maybe even arrest Uncle. Adam Green, after all, was deeply involved with Portia, Junior, and the alien artifact.

Percy began pacing in tighter circles. Portia and the Green Man had seen this behavior before and knew he was coming up with a plan, so they didn't bother him. Now, Percy thought, the key to stopping Tono was the silver cylinder. It wouldn't be enough for her just to discover it wasn't an alien artifact. She'd just think she'd been tricked, and the artifact had been hidden somewhere else. She'd still be after the Green Man, Uncle, and Portia for hiding it. She'd have to find it in a way that would make her look like a fool.

"She'd find it and then reveal it to everybody, with Lou Lonewolf, Uncle, and Portia, and everybody right there!"

"What are you talking about?" asked Becky, a little bewildered by Percy's behavior.

"I've got a plan, and if it works, it will solve everything. First of all, we need to call Uncle and have him and Barney go to the exhibit hall. We'll have them whisper to everybody that there's going to be a special announcement at Becky's book signing. Tell them to also tell Lou Lonewolf, if they can find him. That way Tono is bound to hear about it and know that Becky will appear. Remember, she wants to question Becky, too. Several minutes after Becky is supposed to start her book signing, all of us will show up with her. Now here's what we'll do . . ."

183

Meanwhile, Tom had raced back to the exhibit hall, hoping to get there before Tono realized he was gone. She was just coming out the door when he reached the lobby.

"I was just in the restroom," he explained. "I didn't see any of them."

"I didn't either. Let's go to Becky Moon's room. She's up to her nose in this, too. That Junior Green and Percy are probably both with her. They're all involved in an extraterrestrial cover-up! I can feel it in my bones. Adam, Junior, and Portia are aliens; I know it. And that Becky Moon, she's not an alien – she too weird to be an alien – but I'll tell you what; I think she is some sort of go-between. She's a messenger between different alien groups, and that silver cylinder is her communication device! Adam or one of the other aliens gave it to her so that she can keep in touch with them when they are not at these conventions!

Now, something has happened and she's going to expose all the aliens she is working with!"

"But that doesn't make any sense!" Tom said.

"Shut up; you're an idiot!" snapped Tono.

The hair on the back of Tom's neck stood on end. He couldn't stand the thought of anything happening to Becky. There was no question in his mind now. Tono was ready for the looney bin. "Listen," he pleaded, "don't you think we should be a little cautious. We really don't have any proof of anything; and if we are mistaken, it will discredit the department, and we may both lose our jobs."

"I'm not wrong about this, Tom. These conventions have gone on too long! They are a breeding ground for conspiracies to take over the earth! Now is my big chance to prove it. I'll take full responsibility for everything and full credit, too. You just stay with me and out of the way. Come on, let's go to Becky's room!"

Meanwhile behind one of the open doors to the exhibit hall stood Lou Lonewolf. He had slipped out of sight a few minutes before, and Tono hadn't noticed he was gone. He heard all that she said. "What a story!" he thought, as he listened. If I'm careful, I'll be there when she captures a bunch of extraterrestrials, plus an alien artifact, and I won't need Tono's permission to publish it if it all happens in a public area!" He followed them to Becky's room and hid in the stairwell.

Tono pounded on the door, but, of course, no one was there to answer. She yelled and threatened, but no one answered. She was sure Becky was in there, so she forced hotel management to open the door. She was even more furious when she found no one there. Tom was relieved. Lou was delighted, as he made notes of what she had done for his blog.

The frustrated Tono now stomped back to the

185

exhibit hall, telling Tom that one of her aliens was bound to show up there before the convention was over. When the two arrived, there was a lot of whispering and excitement among the crowd. Lou was right behind them and was immediately accosted by the Beamus twins.

"Have you heard the news?" Casper asked him, and then, without waiting for an answer, said, "Becky's going to make an announcement at her book signing. She hinted about something in her talk yesterday, remember? Everybody thinks it has to be about the alien artifact."

"We know it is, because we've seen it," whispered Pollox. "We won't tell you how we've seen it, but will say that we also, briefly, had it in our possession."

He sounded sad and disappointed, and Lou knew why, for he had seen Junior Green take the silver cylinder away from them. What he wondered was, if Becky now had the silver cylinder back, how did she get it? "This story," he said to himself, "gets stranger and stranger. What did it all mean? First Becky has the cylinder, then the Beamus twins have it, then Junior Green has it, now Becky has it back. Stranger and stranger! Somehow all these people must be part of a conspiracy!"

The twins turned and made their way toward the raised platform at the back of the hall where Becky was to do her book signing. They wanted to be up close when the cylinder was revealed. They doubted

186

it could now be of any benefit to them, but, still, there was a chance.

It wasn't long before Tono and Tom had heard the news, and they, too, made their way to the platform. Tono was gloating, knowing she was going to make an arrest. Tom was in a panic, powerless to stop her. He wished he could get to Becky before she appeared, but Tono wouldn't let him leave her side. He wished he knew what she was going to say. He didn't know what the cylinder actually was, but Becky said it was nothing important. If that were so, why should she reveal it? And if it were something important, why had she lied to him about it? It was all a mystery to him, but whatever happened, he wasn't going to let Tono arrest this girl!

Gradually all the exhibit booths were abandoned, and people collected around the low platform. It was 12:00, and Becky hadn't yet appeared. People began whispering to one another. Had something happened? Did Becky's spaceship come back for her?

Suddenly at 12:10 there was a stir in the front of the hall, and the crowd parted as Becky Moon entered, followed by Portia, Percy, Pouncer, the Green Man, Uncle, and Barney. They stepped onto the platform and lined up behind the desk piled with copies of Becky's book, *By Invitation*. Becky picked up the microphone on the desk.

"Hello, everyone," she began. "Before we begin the book signing, I want to say something. I mentioned in my talk yesterday that I had something special to announce, but then the lights went out before I could explain. As you know, rumors have been running through the convention that an alien artifact was going to be revealed, and some people supposed, for reasons I won't explain, that I was the one who was going to do it. In fact, I did have an announcement to make, but the power went out before I could do it. During the power outage I went to my room, and I discovered it had been searched, and something was taken from it, a silver cylinder."

Excited murmurs ran through the crowd. "I won't say who took it, but they didn't get far before they were stopped by two of the people behind me, Junior and Percy Green. They retrieved the cylinder. Somehow the knowledge that I possessed this cylinder got out, and certain people came to believe that it was the alien artifact, and the thing my announcement was to be about. What I want to tell everyone is that the silver cylinder is not an alien artifact and has nothing to do with my announcement. I now want to say that what I was going to announce is no longer relevant, and I'm sorry to say that I don't have an alien artifact. I wish I had."

Ohs and ahs of disappointment swept through the hall. As they did so, Janet Tono lurched onto the platform, reluctantly followed by Tom Gerry. "Just a minute here," roared Tono. "You think you can get away with a simple explanation like that? That won't do, my girl! There's much more to the story than you're telling! I want that silver cylinder, and I want it now!"

She pushed Becky away from the mic and, glaring at her, held out her hand. "Hand it over," she demanded.

The audience was thrilled. They all knew who Janet Tono was, and many had heard about Adam Green's relatives visiting the convention, so Junior, Portia and Percy were not unknown. Now they expected to find that the silver cylinder was indeed an alien artifact. The Green Man reached in his shoulder bag and drew it out. Everyone craned to see it. The silver object gleamed in the spotlight shining down on the platform.

"In the name of the Department of Homeland Security, I'm confiscating this alien object, and I'm detaining all of you on this platform as risks to national security for keeping it from me. I also believe that Portia Green is an extraterrestrial, and at least some of the rest of you are also!" Tono shouted.

A roar of shock and surprise thrilled through the crowd. This was the highlight of the convention and something they would remember all their lives and tell their grandkids. So it was an actual alien artifact after all, and not only that, but actual alien to go with it!

"But it's not an alien artifact," protested Becky. "It's mine, and it's something personal! Open it, you'll

189

see!"

Janet Tono looked at Becky and then at the crowd. She wouldn't open it; she couldn't open it. What if it did something when she opened it? What if it exploded or dissolved her, or who knows what? Besides, she couldn't reveal an alien artifact to this crowd of UFO nuts. It would breech national security. And then, in the very unlikely chance that it wasn't an alien artifact and she opened it, she would look like a fool. She'd be disgraced; she'd never live it down. No, she wouldn't open it. She'd let the experts at Area 51 open it. Yes, she would let them handle it, and this alien bunch behind her, too!

Percy was in a sweat. His whole plan hinged on Tono opening the silver cylinder. "It's not working!" he whispered to Portia. "She's got to open it!"

"Open it!" declared Portia.

"No!" shouted Tono. "I won't open it. It would breach national security!"

"Open it!" roared the crowd.

At this moment Pouncer crept forward and quickly tried to wiggle his way between Tono's legs, remembering the effect he had on her the night before. In her agitated state that was all it took to send her over the edge of sanity. She let out a blood-curdling scream and tossed the cylinder in the air! As if in slow motion, it performed several somersaults and hit the edge of the table. The end popped off, and out flew a slender cut glass bottle containing an amber liquid.

190

The bottle shot into the crowd. A young woman caught it and held it above her head, laughing.

"Look!" she shouted, "it's perfume! It's a bottle of *Hidden Secret* perfume!"

Riotous laughter rolled through the hall. Sure, everybody thought, it wasn't an alien artifact, but what a joke on that loony Tono. Tono herself couldn't help the purple on her face spreading to her ears, neck, and down her arms. She looked wildly around. She couldn't take all these people to Area 51 for having a bottle of perfume!

"Come on, Tom," she shrieked, and tottered off the platform. "I've been tricked! These evil aliens set me up! Let's check out of this lunatic asylum before they do something deadly to me!"

Tom didn't move. "No," he shouted back. "I quit!"

Janet Tono turned and glared at him but didn't argue. It was just as well, she thought. Tom was too dumb to be a Homeland Security agent. She pushed her way through the conventioneers, knocking people about like a human bowling ball. No more than five minutes elapsed before she checked out.

After the crowd settled down, Becky went forward with her book signing. The publisher had sent a hundred copies for her to sell and autograph, but that wasn't nearly enough. Many people went away disappointed. Some had the foresight to bring their copy from home, and everybody she talked to was thrilled with how the convention went. They weren't at all disappointed that a real alien artifact didn't appear. Some even asked her if she had started the rumor just to trick and humiliate Janet Tono. Many said they couldn't wait for the next convention and asked if she were coming. All the while she signed, Tom Gerry stood behind her, handing her copies and smiling.

By 3:00 all the books were gone and the exhibits closed. Uncle, Barney, the Green Man, Portia, Percy, Pouncer, Becky, and Tom gathered in Uncle's suite on the 10th floor. Everyone was exhausted and flopped down on the first chair they came to. Becky and Tom sank into the couch, with Portia beside them. Becky took Tom's hand.

"You lost your job because of me. I'm sorry," she murmured.

"That's okay," said Tom. "I didn't like it very much anyway."

"Maybe you could find another one in Gold Hill, where Becky lives," suggested Portia.

"Hey, you know what?" said Becky. "Our sheriff is looking for a new deputy. The one we have now is going to retire this fall."

Tom squeezed her hand. "That sounds good." He was silent for a minute and then said, "You know what? I really don't understand all the stuff that's happened the past couple of days. It seems to me that your perfume bottle in the pretty case didn't really start all this mix-up. Is there an alien artifact

192

somewhere? And where did you guys disappear to when we searched Becky's room? And are there really some extraterrestrials at this convention?"

No one spoke, and, looking at Becky, he went on. "You know, when Tono and I first came here, I thought you were just a beautiful girl who had made up a book about being visited by a spaceship. I didn't see anything wrong with that. And I thought all these people who came to the convention were just a little bit crazy and had come here just to have fun. Now I'm thinking that your book is true, and this convention wasn't all just fun. I'm thinking there's a lot more going on here than meets the eye. I'm even thinking that, as crazy as Tono is, maybe there's an element of truth in her suspicions."

Becky reached over with her free hand and patted Tom's hand. "It's sometimes better if some things remain a mystery," she observed. "I'm glad that you now believe my book's true, because it is. As far as this convention goes, there were a lot of things going on, but I've promised not to reveal all I know. Maybe sometime in the future you'll know more. And on a spaceship yourself! As I said in my book, I think my alien friends are coming back!"

There was another silence that lasted until broken by Pouncer, who asked if they were ever going to eat. Percy told everyone what he said and Barney got on the phone to order room service. Percy told him to get two cheeseburgers and two fish sandwiches for

193

Pouncer. Becky, after whispering to Tom, said not to order for them. They were going to check out and leave right away for Gold Hill.

"It turned out that I enjoyed this convention, and to begin with I wasn't sure I would," she said. "I'm sorry for any trouble I've caused."

"Hey," exclaimed Uncle, "things have turned out splendidly. We hope to see you at the next convention. You were a great attraction. It will be in Anaheim in February. We've done well enough here that we can plan that far ahead!"

"I'll be there," smiled Becky. "Or maybe *we* will be there."

"Yeah!" added Tom, beaming and looking down at her.

They stood up, shook hands with everyone, scratched Pouncer's ears, and left.

Chapter 16

"All's Well That Ends Well"

"**D**idn't I say," grinned the Green Man, "that Percy Fitz would fix everything? First of all, I wanted him to explain to me all the crazy things that were going on here, and he did that. You wouldn't talk to me," he added, frowning at Uncle, "and Percy fixed that. You lost your MiniGen, and Percy found it. Your business was losing money, and Percy found a way to sell more tickets. 'Tickets,' is that the word? Anyway, he suggested getting the rumor started about the alien artifact. Then there was that horrible creature, Janet Tono. She was going to expose a real alien artifact and throw us all in Area 51, and, instead, Percy exposed her! What is Area 51, anyway? I would call all of that brilliant! Don't I always say that Percy is brilliant?"

"You're giving me too much credit," blushed Percy. "It was really all of us together that did those things, and if it hadn't have been for Pouncer tripping up Tono, who knows what would have happened!"

"Yeah," whistled Pouncer. "I'm brilliant, too! When I saw she wasn't going to open it, I knew I was the only one who could save the day! Besides, I wanted to trip her again anyway. That's the most fun I've had on this adventure, except maybe getting my ears and tail painted black."

"The only thing remaining," murmured the Green Man, looking at Uncle, "is getting Uncle to return to Kolobro with me. I don't suppose you've got any ideas left to accomplish that, do you Percy?"

"Now, listen, my boy," said Uncle, before Percy could admit he hadn't. "I haven't been away that long, not in our way of keeping time. And I would have come back for a brief visit if my Transporter Gens hadn't disappeared. I've been to over a thousand planets, and this planet is a very special place. I've watched it progress over the centuries, and I've come to think of it as home. I like what I do, and Barney Bailey, here, is a great friend. I don't want to leave just yet, but I'll tell you what I want you to do. I want you to bring the entire family here for a visit!"

"That would be great!" beamed the Green Man. "But do you think they would trust me to pilot them here. Did I tell you I got caught in a solid rock mountain trying to get here, and lost one of my Transporter Gens? Thanks to Percy and Portia I got it back, but maybe I won't be so lucky next time. The family will be very cross if I trap them in solid rock. And, remember, even you, a master planet pilot, had trouble coming here."

"I've been thinking about that over the years," said Uncle, "about how the Transporter Gens separated from the room, and it's still a mystery to me how it happened. It's just something strange about this planet. So, although I don't know what causes it, I have figured out a way to prevent it from happening. Before you leave, I'll write down some special instructions and additional settings for your Transporter Gens that I think will prevent the problem."

"Maybe you should put a couple of extra Transporter Gens in your shoulder bag," whispered Portia to the Green Man. He nodded at her and then exclaimed, "Well, you've done it again, Percy! The whole family is going to be together!"

"Green Man," protested Percy, rolling his eyes, "I didn't do it!"

"Never mind," said Portia, taking Percy's arm, "when you're around, things just happen! But now I think it's time for us to go home. I know that Janet Tono has left, but what if she comes back looking for me? I'm not an extraterrestrial, but she knows I'm not a normal girl, and she may try to track me down. I'd feel more comfortable if we were back in Aurora, and I don't mean Aurora, Colorado!"

"That sounds good to me!" agreed Percy.

"You know," added Portia, "there is one other thing I wish we could have done something about. Those Beamus twins. Not only are they still a possible threat to Uncle and Barney, but I feel sorry for them, being stranded here and wanting to go home. I mean we get to go home, but they don't."

"You know what just occurred to me?" beamed the Green Man, with a broad smile. "Why don't I take those two home? If there were only a way of determining the coordinates of their planet, I could drop them off on my way to Kolobro. Even if it's out of my way, it can't be that far from Earth, seeing how they got here by spaceship!"

"That's a great idea, Junior!" exclaimed Uncle. "Between me and the Beamus boys, we could figure out the coordinates, and I could set them on Junior's Transporter Gens. I suspect they're from somewhere in the constellation of Cancer, and that's on your way. I'll tell you what, Junior, you take Portia, Percy, and Pouncer home, then come back. I'll get the Beamuses here, and we'll figure everything out!"

"I say!" the Green Man chuckled, "this is fabulous! Even I get to be the solution to a problem. I can't wait to tell everyone on Kolobro all my adventures and how I did something splendid!"

After an early supper at which Pouncer got his cheeseburgers and fish, the Green Man gave Uncle one of his extra MiniGens and kept the broken one to take back for repair. He told Uncle that it was too bad he hadn't carried several extras with him in the first place. Uncle smiled and said that he had gotten so used to his successful visits to planets, that he never thought he would need an extra MiniGen; but in the future he would take Junior's advice and always carry an extra. He reminded Junior to hurry back. ("Hurry" was probably nowhere near as fast on Kolobro as it is on Earth.) Then he and Barney escorted them to a vacant spot in the back of the hotel parking lot.

Goodbyes were said by all. There was a bright light and a popping sound, and the Green Man, Portia, Percy, and Pouncer found themselves in the courtyard of the Aurora castle.

"Percy, you're a wonder," said the Green Man, shaking his hand violently. "If ever I get in trouble again, no matter where I am, I'll come get you!"

"Well," said Percy, alarmed, "remember that now you've found Uncle, he can probably help you much better than I can!"

"Portia," said the Green Man, ignoring Percy's comment, "you, too, are a wonder. I saw how you got those two love birds to stay together – suggesting that maybe Tom could find a job in Becky's town. I saw what you were doing! And the Beamus twins, too, you brought up the idea to help them out!"

"What about me?" complained Pouncer.

"You're the most wonderful of all," grinned the Green Man. "You tripped old Tono up twice! Twice, mind you!"

Pouncer bristled up and strutted in a circle. "Percy, don't tell Mom and Dad I stowed away in the transporter room. Just tell 'em how I tripped up old Tono!"

The Green Man hugged all three, adjusted his Transporter Gens for a return trip to the Desert Wind Hotel and Convention Center, and, with a bright light and a pop, was gone.

It was the night cycle in Aurora when they arrived, so the only other people to witness their arrival were the two guards at the castle gate. They snapped to attention and ran forward, their beetled-like armor clanking, to greet the trio of travelers. They wanted to ring the alarm bell and alert the whole city to their return. (Word that they had embarked on an adventure to the Outworld had not remained a castle secret.) Portia wouldn't allow it, however. She said people would find out soon enough, and she didn't want to disturb their sleep.

As they walked to the bedchamber of King Priam and Queen Penelope, Portia sighed, "I suppose we will have to have a council meeting and describe our adventure to everyone, and have Bartelo, the scribe, write it all down to be included in the history of Aurora. And I suppose we should also have Shakescene, the poet, there as well. The people will demand he write a play and a long poem about it. You know how excited they get about our adventures."

"Don't forget to tell everybody how I tripped up old Tono, two times!" whistled Pouncer with a yawn.

"The only thing is," said Percy, "how do we explain to everybody what happened? I mean, it's one thing to explain that the Green Man came from another planet, like we did when he first came here, but how do we explain about UFO conventions, and people dressing up like space aliens, and the Department of Homeland Security. The people of Aurora won't understand that stuff."

"That's true," agreed Portia, "but you'll think of some way to make it understandable. You always come up with a solution."

"Yeah, and you always say that!" grumbled Percy.

Chapter 17

Lou Lonewolf's Blog

Desert Wind Hotel and Convention Center, Phoenix, Arizona.

The tenth annual UFO convention for the Southwest area wound up today with a surprise, but not the one the participants expected. As you will recall from my blog entry of several days ago, there was a rumor circulating through the rooms, halls, and exhibits that an alien artifact was to be revealed sometime before the convention ended.

The word spread like the huge and mysterious dust storm that enveloped this city last night. Registrations grew to double what we normally see at these conventions, and there were even some very unusual participants, and that's saying something; for, as you know, not your normal crowd come to these things!

There were people dressed in all the usual sorts of costumes one would expect. But new this year were outfits depicting the characters in that smash bestseller, *By Invitation*, Becky Moon's description of her encounter with alien beings. Among those dressed up like these alien beings was a strikingly beautiful girl named Portia Green. She claimed to be the niece of one of the convention sponsors, Adam Green. Along with her, and also in costume, were an ordinary-looking boy named Percy Green and a very large cat called Pouncer. Then there was a handsome young man, not in costume, named Junior Green. All of these people claimed to be related to Adam Green, but I suspect that is not entirely true. (More on this in a later blog.)

You are probably asking yourself why I am mentioning these people. It's because these supposed relatives of Mr. Green appear to be at the heart of all the strange happenings.

After the rumor of an alien artifact had reached all ears at the convention, Becky Moon was giving a talk about the events that led to her writing her book. Toward the end of her speech she started to make an announcement. Everyone held their breath, thinking this was it. She was going to reveal something about the alien artifact. At that very moment the dust storm hit, and the lights and power went out. Strange, don't you think? Of all the moments when a storm hits and the power goes off, it's the moment when, perhaps, the biggest announcement in human history is to be made – the actual public revealing of an object from another planet!

Of course, the announcement was not made, and my investigations led me through the dark corridors of the hotel to a spot outside Becky Moon's room. My reporter's instincts led me there, and I was not disappointed. I watched as two individuals somehow forced the lock and went inside. For now, I choose not to reveal who these two individuals are because they may be part of a different, but related, story I'm pursuing. I will simply call them C and P.

After a few minutes they exited the room. One of them had a bulge in his pocket that wasn't there when he entered the room! This, I said to myself, this must be the alien artifact! After hearing Becky Moon's speech, these men had rushed to her room and stolen it before she could return!

They went down the hall, and I followed. Now, my dear readers, things got even more mysterious. Not far down the hall they encountered Percy and Junior Green. I doubt that this was a coincidence! Had Percy and Junior planned to search Becky Moon's room, too? As I watched in the dimness, for only the emergency lights were on, they stopped C and P and forced them to give up the thing in C's pocket. From what I could see in the dim light, it was a silver cylinder about eight or ten inches long and two or three inches in diameter. How did they know C had it? I can testify that they didn't see C and P leave Becky's room. Could that cat, Pouncer, who was with them, somehow detect it? If so, how? There's no denying he isn't a normal house cat. In any case, they forced C and P to give up the cylinder. I then followed Percy and Junior Green, but lost them in a crowd.

What happened to the silver cylinder after that, I can't say. What I will say is this. I suspect, because of what happened later, that the cylinder was opened and the alien artifact removed! The next day, after all these events had occurred, and the lights and power had come back on, Becky Moon came to the exhibit hall to sign books. She walked onto the platform, followed by Adam, Junior, Percy, and Portia Green, and Barney Bailey, along with their strange, oversized kitty. Becky was obviously nervous as she took the microphone and began to speak before signing any books. She faltered and muttered something about not having an alien artifact. At this point, Janet Tono, that Department of Homeland Security agent that haunts all UFO gatherings, and who all my readers know for her staking habits and threatening ways, rushed forward, said that she knew Junior Green had a silver cylinder, and demanded that he give it to her. She shouted that it was an alien artifact, and she was confiscating it and arresting all the Green family, as well as Barney Bailey and Becky Moon, as risks to national security. She also shouted that the lovely girl, Portia, was an extraterrestrial!

At this point the crowd shouted for her to open the silver cylinder. She refused, and as she walked to the edge of the platform that strange cat that the Greens called Pouncer dived between her legs! I tell you it was no accident. That cat knew exactly what it was doing! One has to ask, is that really a cat, or

205

something else?!

Tono shrieked in terror and the silver cylinder flew from her hands, hit a chair, and popped open. Out flew not an alien artifact but a bottle of perfume! I tell you, my loyal readers, it was a setup! Those Greens intimidated Becky. They took the alien artifact and made Becky replace it with the perfume! They did it for two reasons: they didn't want the artifact revealed, and they wanted to discredit Janet Tono. She was getting too close to the truth! They accomplished both!

Here's my theory. Becky Moon did, indeed, have an alien artifact. How she got it, I don't know, but it's somehow connected with the aliens she describes in her book. Junior and Portia Green, and that cat, Pouncer, are, indeed, extraterrestrials! They look just like the ones described in Becky's book! (Of course, Junior had dyed his hair.) How the boy, Percy, fits in, I don't know, but these three somehow talked their way into having Adam Green say they were relatives. They confronted Becky and made her say the alien artifact was only a silver cylinder with her perfume in it. I suspect they promised her more alien spaceship rides!

Now, what makes my theory even more plausible is what happened next. After the convention ended, I went up to Adam Green's suite to confront him and his supposed relatives about my theory. He said that Junior, Portia, Percy, and Pouncer had just left. I rushed from the suite and, when I didn't see them in the lobby, ran to the parking lot. I spotted them at the far end of the lot, walking toward an area where there were no cars. I ran as fast as I could, but by the time I got to where they were, they had disappeared! I mean that literally! There were no cars in that area. There was a high cinder block wall on the border of the lot. There was no place they could have gone! I tell you, my loyal readers, they just DISAPPEARED!

Whatever the alien artifact was I don't suppose we will ever know! I doubt that we will ever see that fake Green family again either. Later, when I went back and questioned Adam Green, he refused to talk about his so-called relatives. He even accused me of imagining some of the things that happened! You, my readers, know better!

I end my story by telling everyone, and I mean everyone, who attends these conventions in the future; watch closely! Watch everything and everyone! Because there may be more Green family members and more aliens and alien artifacts among us than we realize! Remember, KEEP WATCH!

AFTERWORD

For those of you who haven't read the other Percy Fitz books, and for those of you who have but have forgotten, there is a character named Rufus McGee. Rufus has an old trailer in Pan Woods and joined Percy and Portia on two of their adventures. He always suspected Portia of being an extraterrestrial, and she and Percy had never claimed she wasn't. And, furthermore, he had, in fact, once seen a flying saucer hovering above his trailer.

Now, Rufus spends part of each year at a trailer court not many miles east of Phoenix. Two days after the convention ended, he was sitting outside his new motor home (He bought it with the gold and jewels Portia and Percy had given him.), drinking his morning freshly-squeezed orange juice and reading the newspaper. He turned to the local section, gasped, and spilled juice all down his dingy white t-shirt, even splashing some onto his always smudgy glasses. There was a photo and article on the 10th Annual UFO Convention - Southwest Area. What amazed and astounded poor Rufus was the photo of the exhibit hall, for there, clearly to be seen among the many participants, was Portia, and next to her with his face partially hidden by somebody in an alien costume, was none other than Percy Fitz!

"Great gobs of boiled owl!" exclaimed Rufus. "What adventure are they up to their necks in now?" He brushed the orange juice off his shirt and pants. "Whatever it is, and as much as I like them, I'm glad they didn't invite me! Those two get in the most terrible fixes, and I'm too old to rescue them again!"

THE END?
MAYBE – MAYBE NOT

About the Author

After earning a Bachelor of Arts degree in English and a master's degree in library and information science, he worked for many years as a librarian. He now spends part of his time at his cabin in the mountains of central Utah, where he hikes, reads, writes and tells "mostly true" stories to his wife, children and grandchildren.